USA TODAY BESTSELLING AUTHOR
ALLYSON LINDT

For my eternal dragon

Chapter One

"Nothing's out of place, I promise." Mercy smoothed an invisible strand of hair for her best friend, and met her gaze in the mirror. She patted down another non-existent strand—though she wasn't sure if it was to reassure Liz or herself.

"I know. I just—" Liz stood and paced from one end of the hotel room to the other, the long train of her wedding dress draped over one arm, to keep from dragging. "You know?"

"I do. I get it." Or, Mercy understood the theory. It was Liz's wedding day. Liz had met an amazing man—who happened to be almost as painfully wealthy as she was—and was pledging to spend the rest of her life with him. Of course she was nervous. Mercy couldn't see herself making this kind of commitment, but most girls dreamed of this day, and Liz's had been planned to perfection.

Big, but not too big. A dress worth more than Mercy's battered Honda. An all-day gala in Salt Lake's greatest and grandest five-star hotel. A skiing honeymoon in Park City, a gift courtesy of Liz's brother.

The groom didn't have any family, and Liz only invited those closest to her. Mercy and Liz grew up in Park City, about twenty-five miles from their current location, and while Mercy couldn't wait to get out of the state when she turned eighteen, Liz stayed where life was familiar. She said she'd moved around enough as a kid, and she wanted some stability.

George offered that. God, had they really only dated for six months?

Mercy grabbed Liz's wrist, to stop her. "You're about to spend all day on your feet. Sit."

"I can't. I'd rather breathe right now."

The dress was tight. And hand-beaded. Flowing lace and satin. This George guy really let Liz go all out. Mercy hadn't met him yet—she'd flown in late last night—but if Liz loved him, he had to be special.

"Think about something else. Anything. Like all the incredible sex you're going to have on your honeymoon," Mercy said.

Liz laughed, and her spine seemed less rigid than seconds earlier. "Do you think we can get away with doing it on a gondola?"

"Like you're going to leave your room long enough to ski? We both know you'll be screwing like bunnies for the next ten days."

"You're so right. He does this thing with his tongue—"

"No details." Mercy didn't have a problem with the graphic conversation, but Liz got this kind of sweet, sappy longing in her voice whenever she brought up doing it with George, and it pinged something inside that Mercy refused to acknowledge.

Liz stuck out her tongue. "Prude."

"Yeah, okay. That's me." They both knew Mercy was anything but. She'd founded her company, Graceful Exhibition Advertising, on the tagline *Grow your adult website to impressively visible sizes.*

Liz's smile faded into something more serene, and she looked Mercy in the eye. "Thank you so much for being here."

"Of course. I wouldn't miss it for anything. Plus, this dress is gorgeous." She gestured at her fitted blue satin gown. Elegant instead of gaudy. It hugged her body and almost gave her curves.

"I'm being serious, Mel."

From anyone else, the nickname summoned bad memories. From Liz, it made Mercy smile. "Me too. I can tell you're happy, and you deserve it." Even if she weren't looking forward to the chance of hooking up with one of the groom's friends after the reception, and despite the fact she put a client proposal on hold for a couple of days to be here, Mercy wouldn't have things any other way. Liz had earned a little joy in her life, and this was a good start.

Someone knocked and seconds later said, "Liz, it's me."

Mercy's blood turned to ice in her veins. Ian was Liz's older brother; he was giving away the bride. Mercy knew he'd be here, but she'd hoped to keep the interaction to a minimum.

Liz shuffled across the floor double time and yanked the door open. "Get in here. What's up?" She shut off the rest of the world as soon as he stepped inside.

This wasn't fair. Mercy tried not to look. Wasn't going to stare. Twelve years—that made him thirty, for Hell's sake—and he looked a billion times better than she remembered. Which was saying a lot. Dark hair the same color as Liz's barely brushed his ears. His sturdy jaw was clenched. And if most men looked amazing in a tux, regardless of their normal appearance, his elevated him to a god-like status. Or she was exaggerating the tiniest bit. Maybe only Greek-hero level. But not like Hercules or anyone impressive. A minor hero no one heard of, like Actaeon.

His gaze lingered on Mercy, tracing her frame, and her cold skin heated to scorching. He shook his head, as if to rattle something loose, and turned back to Liz. "You're going to want to sit down for this."

"I'm not sitting until I absolutely have to." Liz tapped her stocking toes on the carpet. "What's up?"

"No, really. You need to sit, and you need to breathe. Undo a couple buttons on the dress if you have to." Ian's voice took on a hard edge.

"With a lead-in like that, you know you've killed whatever potency your news has, right?" Mercy tried to keep her tone light, despite the concern creeping into her gut.

He gave her a weak smile that didn't reach his eyes.

Liz grabbed his arm. "Stop. Tell me what you want."

"There was a disturbance outside. Hotel security stopped it, but a couple of the guests caught it on camera, and now the video making its way around the party." He held up his phone for Liz to see.

Silence stretched into the room. Sounds filtered from the tiny speakers. Mercy struggled to make out the crackling voice, but she caught phrases like *I'm his wife*, and *already married,* and *you'll pay, you fucking whore.*

Liz sank to the floor. A series of tiny noises, like stitches tearing, mingled with her *Oh, fuck me.*

"Was that what I think it was?" Mercy asked.

Ian pocketed his phone. "George Debson's wife showed up and started screaming about how Liz would never get away with marrying him. She'd lose everything. You caught the gist of it."

The pit in Mercy's gut filled with lead. It was a lot of information to process, for so few words. She watched Liz, concern growing as emotions flashed across her best friend's face before it hardened into a stone mask.

Mercy knelt next to her. "Liz? Talk to me. Say *something.*" It wasn't the silence that bothered her so much as the cold steel reflected in Liz's gaze.

*

The one thing that distracted Ian from how drop-dead-fuckable Mercy looked in that dress—she was a dangerous temptation in her late teens, and this was a hundred times that—was Liz crumbling at the news she'd more or less been left at the altar. By a married man. At least when fate stuck the knife in, she twisted it hard enough to maim. Ian asked Liz when she got engaged to let him run a background check on the guy. Several times. She insisted they were in love and she trusted her fiancé. But *I told you so* could wait.

"Help me up." Liz held one arm toward Ian and the other toward Mercy. Her tone was eerily flat, and her expression matched. They tugged her to her feet, and she turned her back to Mercy. "Get me out of this thing."

Mercy was already undoing the dozens of tiny pearl buttons along Liz's dress, one at a time. "Damage control. What's on the list?"

"The guests already have an idea what's going on." Liz looked at Ian. He nodded. "Then someone needs to go out there and explain, and apologize," she said.

"I'll do it." Mercy grabbed a robe off the back of a nearby chair and handed it over. "You get more comfortable clothes, and then we can deal with catering and other staff."

The brisk tones creeped Ian out, because they meant Liz was shutting this away, to deal with later. At the same time, the synchronization between the two women was amazing. He knew they hadn't seen much of each other all these years, despite their keeping in touch. It was hard to meet up, when Mercy refused to set foot back in the state before now.

But this exchange, both what they said and the words hidden between the lines, had the same smooth rhythm they shared when they were teenagers.

"Wait. You said she mentioned losing everything." Liz looked at Ian. "Do you think she knows where the condo is?"

"You're safer guessing *yes* than assuming *no*."

"Shit. All my stuff is there."

Of course it was. She moved in with George almost immediately after he proposed.

"You've got your luggage for the honeymoon, so it's not all your stuff." Mercy lifted her skirt enough to put on a pair of matching heels that made her grow almost to Ian's height. "And you can always buy more."

He wouldn't stare at Mercy's long legs. Shouldn't acknowledge the way the satin stretched over her ass when she bent at the waist. Refused to follow the path of her hands when she straightened and smoothed her palms down her stomach. He stashed the thoughts. "I'll head over to condo, Liz, and make sure your stuff is safe. See if I can grab a couple of guys to help me clear your things out before someone else does."

"Thanks." Mercy gave him a tiny smile, gratitude in her eyes.

Someone else knocked. "Excuse me, Ms. Thompson? Hotel management."

Liz twirled her finger in the air, gesturing for Ian to turn around. He did, and the rustle of fabric reached his ears. Seconds later, she said, "Okay, let him in."

He glanced over his shoulder, to see she'd pulled on the terrycloth robe and cinched it tight.

Ian opened the door, and a short gentleman stepped into the room. Another man stood in the hallway, arms crossed. "Ms. Thompson, I know this is a special day for you, and I'm sorry to interrupt"— the manager's tone lacked sincerity—"but given the recent news, and that your fiancé's card was declined, payment for your reservations needs to be re-secured."

"Are you fucking kidding me?" Ian's disbelief slipped out before he could stop it. "Do you have any tact?"

"I do. I also have a hotel to run, and a thousands-of-dollars' bill that's about to go delinquent." The manager looked at him.

Liz's chin quivered, and Ian realized her fragile façade was seconds from cracking. "My company has an account with this chain. We'll switch the bill to our name," he said.

"That's nice." The manager sounded as if it were anything but. "Do you want me to charge that to I-don't-believe-you-dot-com?"

Ian pulled his wallet out, extracted a business card and a company credit card, and handed them to the man. "I'd like to you charge Thompson Advertising. Can we have this conversation someplace more private? I believe my sister has more important things to deal with."

The manager's demeanor shifted in an instant, at the sight of the black American Express card. "Of course. My office is down the hall."

Ian turned back to Mercy and Liz. "I'll call you and let you know what I find out about the condo." He grabbed Mercy's arm. "Can I borrow you for a second?" He tried and failed to ignore the rush of heat at the contact, as well as the quick gritting of her teeth before her expression slid back to neutral.

She looked at Liz, who nodded. "Yeah," Mercy said. She followed him into the hallway.

"Keep an eye on her." It wasn't a request, and he knew Mercy would anyway, but he needed the reassurance. Ian and Liz's parents died when Liz was nineteen, in the same accident that stole her high school sweetheart and baby girl from her. She'd withdrawn for years.

"Of course. After we're done here, I'm taking her back to my hotel room," Mercy said.

"Thank you. Give me your number, and I'll text or call with any news."

She spat out the digits, glancing over her shoulder at Liz. He typed in her information and sent her a note. She jumped and spun back toward him when a chime echoed from a distant location in the room.

"That's me," he said. "Now you have my number too. I'll drop everything if I have to."

"I know. And I mean it, thank you." Mercy chewed her lip. How was that tempting, in the midst of this bedlam? Maybe the stress was getting to him.

He gave her one more nod, before following the hotel manager to his office. Liz's whirlwind engagement to George had brought her back to life. If this guy broke his baby sister, Ian swore he'd hunt the bastard down, and make him suffer.

Chapter Two

Ian parked on the street in front of the condo Liz had shared with George. He'd called on a few friends. They'd meet him here, and with any luck, Liz's belongings would be secured in an hour or so.

He took the elevator to her floor and stepped off. The hallway was empty. He rounded the corner, and halfway down—right in front of Liz's door— crouched a man with a toolbox. Shit. He was changing the locks.

Ian quickened his pace, until he reached the condo. "Excuse me." He wasn't going to get mad at this person. This wasn't their fault. "What are you doing?"

"Not that it's any of your business, but what do you think?" The guy never looked up from his work.

"I need to get in there, first." Ian stepped forward.

The locksmith rose and blocked his path, hand on his hip. "There tends to be a reason people want locks changed. I don't know you from a Liberty Park bum, so unless you're here with the lady who hired me, you're not getting in. And she's got a key."

"It's my sister's place." Irritation surged inside, mingling with the knowledge he couldn't do anything but try and talk through this. "Her things are in there."

"Oh yeah, you mean the poor gal caught in the middle of this mess?"

Ian wasn't prepared for that. "How do you…?"

"Not the first time the guy's done it. Not the first time his wife's come to me." The locksmith returned to his work. "Which also means, I still can't let you in. Sorry. The woman pays cash and tips well. I'm not losing her as a client."

Ian clenched his fist silently cursing the back of the man's head. If he were more stubborn, maybe he'd sit and argue, or storm the door. "It's all right. I'll be back with my lawyer."

"Your call, pal. Not my problem. Wife's name's on the deed." The locksmith never turned around.

Fuck. This was one more thing Liz didn't need right now. Ian tried to keep his calm as he headed back downstairs. He fished out his phone to tell his friends with the van *not yet.* Wow, sometimes being adult and mature sucked.

He needed to let Liz know about the delay. And speaking of lawyers, have her talk to his, and ensure she hadn't already signed anything over to George.

He'd give her a few hours to deal with what she already knew, and then they'd discuss next steps.

*

"Home sweet home." Mercy set Liz's suitcase by hotel room sofa. "Take it easy tonight, and we'll figure out the rest in the morning."

Liz stepped up behind her. "I can't believe you're still in that dress." She slid down the zipper.

Mercy felt all her bits relax at once, no longer shaped by the rigid fabric. She let out a long exhale of relief. "I didn't realize I needed that. Thank you. Be right back." She shed the dress as she stepped into the bedroom—thank God for extended suites with a little extra room and privacy—and then yanked on a pair of jeans and a sweater.

Liz held up with a scary kind of grace and elegance through the entire evening, apologizing to guests, thanking people as they left, loading gifts into the car and promising to return them, and dealing with the catering staff and making sure the food didn't go to waste. It was only a matter of time before something gave and Liz let the hurt pour in. Mercy'd be there when it happened, even if it meant staying in town another day or two. "What do you want to do now?" she called into the other room.

It made her nervous they hadn't heard from Ian, but if he was retrieving Liz's stuff, that might take a while.

When Liz didn't respond, concern itched under Mercy's skin. "Liz?"

Liz's loud sob felt like a vise clenching around her chest. Mercy rushed back into the living room and found her on the sofa, face buried in her hands, and body shaking. There was the breaking point.

Mercy knelt next to her, wrapped an arm around her shoulder, and pulled her in. "I know. I do, hon."

Soul-shattering cries eventually faded into sniffles and hiccups, punctuated with fragmented thoughts. "I can't believe I didn't see it... All the signs were there... God, this hurts so much... Fucking bastard... Do you think castration is a legal form of punishment? I need a drink. You have booze, right?" She looked up, eyes red and cheeks puffy.

The bill would hurt, but Mercy could suck it up. Especially if she landed this new client. "I have room service." She stood and pulled Liz to her feet. "Wash your face. I'll grab the menu, and we'll see what we can order."

"I don't care, as long as it gets me wasted." Liz's comment faded into running water.

Several hours later, Mercy set the room-service trays outside the room. Between Liz and Mercy, they plowed through nachos, ribs, and meatball subs, and Liz was on her... Mercy didn't even know how many drinks her friend had in her.

Mercy was nursing a watery 7 and 7—her first drink—and telling herself the bill didn't matter. Next month was going to be good for her tiny advertising agency, and this was about Liz's sanity. It was also about keeping Liz from being sick all over the carpet. Mercy snatched the fresh mini bottle, before Liz could pop it open. "Maybe you should have some water."

Liz stuck her tongue out, then giggled. "Yes, Mom." She half-wandered, half-stumbled to the sink and set the glass on the counter with a *thunk* when she was done. "You know what we should do?"

"Put you to bed?"

"Alone? Meh. It's supposed to be my fucking honeymoon."

"I love you, hon, but I'm not sleeping with you."

Liz wrinkled her nose. "You're not my type. Ian, on the other hand, really likes yo—"

"What should we do?" Mercy didn't want to hear that. Talk about reopening old wounds. "You've got a grand and mighty plan, right?"

"Yes. We should go to Park City."

Which was where Ian lived, as did a past Mercy wasn't interested in revisiting. "It's a little late." Nothing was open in this state on a Sunday night.

"I mean tomorrow."

Mercy didn't know if Liz was babbling and drunk, or if she had a point. "You're not much of an outlet-mall shopper. Nordstrom is down the street."

"You're funny. And I'm not that wasted." Liz flopped onto the couch next to Mercy. "You're going with me on my honeymoon. We're going to hop in my car tomorrow morning, drive into the canyons, enjoy impossible levels of snow, and get laid. Every night. Different fucking guy."

"You're sure you're not wasted?"

Liz stared at the ceiling. "Maybe a little. But I'm sick of this. I've been living in a hole for years, trying to get over"—she swallowed—"*them*. And this shit with George… I want to live again and not answer to anyone. Go with me. We'll be stupid for the next ten days and pretend the real world doesn't exist."

That wasn't completely an option. Mercy could take a few days away from work, but she needed to prep this proposal, and she was wooing the client in less than a week. Not that it mattered. Liz's impulse would pass by morning, and Mercy would hop on a plane back to Atlanta. "I'll go with you, but I have to take my laptop."

"Fine. At least you'll keep me company." Liz yawned wide enough, she might dislocate her jaw. "I think I'm sleepy."

"Come on." Mercy helped her stand again. "Drink some more water, and you can go to bed."

Moments later, Liz tumbled onto the mattress in the bedroom. "At least you two love me," she mumbled.

"Always and forever." Mercy squeezed her hand and left her alone to sleep. She was too wired to do the same, but she could watch TV in the other room for a while. A glance at the clock on the nightstand told her it was only nine in the evening. The wedding would have started at five, followed by a full dinner for guests and what would have been a roaring reception, cresting its peak right about now.

This was why Mercy didn't do love. Not the romantic kind, anyway. It always disappointed. From the night Ian left her alone in that stupid mountain town, to every time she or Liz had their hearts torn out, it never redeemed itself. *Fleeting* was fine. A couple days with a guy here, a couple weeks with a girl there... a month with the barista and her husband above the coffee house down the street from The Vatican. Mercy was okay with that, as long as the expiration date was stated or implied.

Maybe Liz was right; a week of debauchery in the mountains was what they both needed. And if they spent most of their time in bars and the hotel, Mercy didn't risk running into her family.

Mercy settled in front of the living room TV and flipped mindlessly through stations. When the text message tone on her phone shattered the calm, she jumped at the sound for the second time that day. Her hammering heart skipped a beat when she saw the message from Ian. Great. The little girl in her wanted to come out and play.

Screw that.

Everything all right? he asked.

Better than it was. Any luck?

News best delivered in person. I'm coming over. Send me your hotel info.

Once upon a time, she would have sold her soul, to get that request from him. Now she forwarded him the address and room number, along with a warning. *She's already asleep.*

Probably for the best. I'm stopping by, anyway.

Presumptuous ass. Of course he was. She sent back a quick, *Swell. I'll be here.*

She resisted the compulsion to check her makeup before he arrived. There was no reason to find something more flattering to wear, either. She didn't need to impress him, and caring what he thought was nothing more than the ghost of a memory. When he knocked, she couldn't help running her fingers through her hair.

Unlike her and Liz, he hadn't changed his clothes. His tie hung loose around his neck, and the top button of his shirt was undone, but he still wore that tuxedo like it was made for him. Who was she kidding? It probably was. Technically they were both in the same industry, but the firm he inherited and expanded was in a different league in both reach and revenue than hers could ever hope to be. And God fuck it, if he didn't look gorgeous in his tux. From a completely clinical perspective, of course. She'd say that about any guy who looked the same.

"She's still sleeping. Probably will be for a while." Mercy didn't angle herself to keep him out, but she didn't invite him in, either.

"Understood. I'm heading back up to Park City tonight. I have to be in the office in the morning. If possible, I'd like to talk to her before then. There were some problems getting her things back. She's going to need to talk to the lawyer."

Mercy winced. Of course it couldn't be easy. What a mess.

Ian nodded behind her. "I'd like to wait, if you don't mind. At least a little while."

"Sure. Not a problem." She stepped aside. She could mention Liz would be heading to the same place he was and he could talk to her then. But Liz might not want her brother knowing she planned on fucking her vacation away—and that was if she still wanted to go once she was sober and hung over. Besides, despite the voice telling Mercy to keep her distance and be cool, the urge to shut Ian out wasn't there. She understood why he did what he had when they were teenagers, and they'd both grown up. Maybe it was time to start over. "I'd offer you something to drink, but we've exhausted most of the good stuff."

He looked over the bottles lined up on the table. "At least she took it well. She is okay, right?" He sat in the middle of the sofa.

Mercy refused to read anything into the action, and took a seat in the armchair next to him. "As well as can be expected. Probably better, considering the circumstances."

"She's lucky you're here."

An awkward silence fell between them. It was better than making a fool of herself, like last time they saw each other. Insisting—at the glorious age of fifteen—she wasn't a child, and that he had to take her with him when he left for college, or she'd go insane, while he gently pushed her aside and told her to go home.

Yup, that was in the past. And sitting in a hotel, trying to look anywhere but at each other, with his sister passed out drunk in the next room, was definitely preferable.

Chapter Three

Ian suspected if discomfort were personified, it would feel a lot like this. Every question he asked, each conversation starter he produced, Mercy knocked back in single syllables.

"How's Atlanta this time of year?"

Nice.

"Any other plans while you're in town?"

No.

"How 'bout that local sports team, huh?" He left the question intentionally vague.

That caused a twitch of her lips. The corners tugged up, and a smile threatened. Good look on her. Then again, everything about her screamed careless seduction. Her faded jeans hugged her ass the way his hands itched to, and her top stopped a few inches short of her waist, leaving a hint of skin exposed and tempting him. Her hair was still pulled up from the wedding, though chunky tendrils escaped and hung down her long neck, and the smudges of mascara under her eyes made him think *freshly fucked.* Or maybe it was studying her and his wishful thinking that did that.

He didn't put any effort into hiding his appraisal of her. Gone was the awkward girl who never left his kid sister's side except to ask Ian some of the most bizarre, insightful, and wonderful philosophical questions he'd heard at that age. This woman was confident, unintentionally elegant, and making his cock jerk every time she licked her lips or brushed her hair out of her face. If his joke got an almost smile from her, could he coax a few more words out, too? "How's business?"

"Good."

There went that idea. He wasn't willing to let it drop so easily. "Rumor is Graceful Exhibition Advertising is doing something new with analytics, and providing ROI charts no one else can match. Curious how you track that on social media."

"You know what I do." She raised her brows.

She was surprised? "I always keep track of what the competition is up to. You're a growing name."

"Growing. Right. Because of our tagline."

"Because you operate on a small budget, maintain a tiny staff who all work remotely, and kick some serious ass in online advertising."

For the first time that evening, she seemed to relax. She sank back in her seat and tucked her legs under her and to the side. "And we help people buy sex."

"Everyone's selling seduction. You're just more honest about it."

"Even you?"

"Even me." He was definitely in the market now, if she was offering. He shook the thought aside. The last thing he wanted was for her to think he didn't take her seriously. He'd watched her company's climb, and regardless of what people thought of her clientele, the woman knew what she was doing. "I'm curious though. Why?" he said.

"Why… adult websites? Be more specific."

"Why advertising? If I knew you were interested, I could have hooked you up."

"No. You couldn't have." Disdain crept into her words. "I didn't set out to do this." And like that, her casual tone returned. "I met this guy when I was in Argentina. He was American too, and we shared a hostel room because it was the only one left. While I was bumming around the world, immersing myself in local culture, he was taking naked pictures of women—for art and posterity—and having them sign release forms. We hit up a few more countries together. Somewhere along the way, he built a website, and I helped him spread the word."

"So, your friend…?"

"Owns Smut Central."

One of the two biggest names in that industry. "You bummed around South America and Europe with Andrew Newton? And you put him on the map?"

She shrugged, but the glint in her eyes radiated more smugness than dismissal. "I played a part in it. I reinvested my share of the money into hiring a couple employees, and you apparently know the rest. Also"—she leaned forward, to rest her elbows on her legs, and her shirt dipped low enough to give him an incredible view of her cleavage—"just because I pimp the product doesn't mean I come with my own price tag."

The conversation kept getting better. This *definitely* wasn't the girl who always hung around the house. "I would never assume that. Or want it."

"No? You're not exactly looking away."

"Don't misunderstand; I want you." Not what he meant to say, but she was still listening, and he liked the potential.

"Because I help people sell sex?"

"What? No. I'm hoping that means you've got an open mind, but if you and I hooked up, it would be because we both wanted it. Nothing to do with money or work."

She looked intrigued rather than upset. "And I become the girl who's in town for one day and gets you off for the night?"

"Or I become the guy you don't have to see again. Works both ways. This would be a mutual agreement." This wasn't like him. Negotiating for sex instead of seducing. She wanted to see his hand, and being up front was a relief.

"Your sister's in the next room."

"You said she'd be out for a while. This is between you and me—unless you're looking for excuses. I won't pressure you if you don't say *yes*."

Her smile turned devilish enough he might as well have seen sexy little horns poking from the top of her head. She caught her bottom lip between her teeth. "What if I like a little pressure?"

"Are you saying yes?" This game was fun. Fuck, her flavor of teasing had him harder than he ever remembered being. When it came to consent though, he wasn't playing blurred-lines games, with her or anyone.

"I'm not letting you strip me down with Liz in the next room," she said.

And that was all Ian needed to hear. Not what he wanted, and certainly not what he hoped for, but she'd given him an answer. "In that case, I'll call her in the morning." He stood, keeping his gaze on Mercy's face despite the temptation to drift it lower. "It was good to see you again, Mercy. Scratch that— it was incredible. Let's do it again in twelve years."

She rose with him and joined him at the door. She offered her hand. A *handshake*, of all fucking things. He preferred a partner, to taking care of business himself, but damn if he wasn't beating off when he got home.

"Have you eaten yet?" he asked.

It wasn't what he was supposed to say. She made herself clear, and he was looking for excuses to extend the evening? *This isn't about getting laid,* his brain argued back. He'd always enjoyed her company without sex, this was his way of not leaving things on a sour note. He regretted how he handled their parting of ways last time. This offer was a way to return things between them to neutral ground. Nothing more.

Why wasn't she replying?

*

Mercy didn't know what she was doing. Since Ian walked in the door, her brain and her words were scattered and out of sync. Instinct told her to slink away from him when the direct conversation started. Change the subject back to something not about sex.

23

As a rule, she didn't cower, flinch, or back down. It kept her in business. The problem with plowing forward when it came to him—with playful banter, then batting his advances aside? His offer was more than just tempting; it was exactly what she wanted, and instead of accepting she turned him down in a flush of pride.

Somehow, she had a second chance. Maybe not at that meaningless fling, but at enjoying his company for another couple of hours. Despite the weight of Liz's drunken room-service binge in her gut, Mercy wasn't ready to tell Ian goodnight. "I could nibble on something." *Ian, preferably.* "Let me leave Liz a note."

She scribbled out a quick, *I'll be back soon. Text me or Ian if you need something,* on hotel stationary and propped it up by the bed. She took another look at Ian, as she joined him, appreciating again how enticing he looked in that suit. "We're not dressed to go to the same type of place." She gestured at herself. "And I don't know if anywhere is open."

"You look incredible. Trust me." He held up his palm. "Ready to go, my lady?"

She settled her hand against his long enough to enjoy the gallant gesture, and tried to be casual about pulling away when they stepped into the hallway. She'd already told him *no*—or close enough. This was nothing more than dinner. Two people with a common friend, catching up.

That was a lie, and not even a very good one. If she could find a way to turn her *no* into a *yes* by the end of the night, without losing face, she was going for it. She was leaving town in the morning or sometime in the next couple of days, so this came with a built-in expiration date.

Ian's SUV was as high end as his suit. She might have made a comment about him compensating, but with the weather where he lived, four- or all-wheel drive was a necessity. The hundred-and-twenty-thousand-dollar price tag the Porsche carried was more of a luxury.

Like Mercy, Ian and Liz were born into money, though Mercy surrendered her inheritance when she left home at eighteen and dropped her family name. Ian earned what he had now, by keeping the family agency alive and thriving after his parents passed. It still left the tiniest hint of resentment inside Mercy. A feeling she didn't like.

The restaurant was tamer than the car, to her relief. A microbrewery with a thinning crowd—given the late hour—but no dress code, and the prices didn't make her wallet recoil in horror. They were seated quickly, at a table with no one else nearby. After the day she had, the quiet was both deafening and saintly. Small talk flowed easily with Ian, but he kept it neutral. They swapped tidbits about the weather, sales software, and industry rumors. Nothing provocative.

It didn't stop her from studying him whenever she had the chance, racking her brain for a way to shift the conversation back to something sexier without looking like she was trying too hard.

Damn it, why had she shut him down?

"Are the two of you ready, or do you need a minute?" The waiter, who introduced himself as Steve, startled Mercy from her musings.

Ian looked at her with expectation. She handed Steve the menu. "Cup of the house soup for me."

Ian raised his brows. "Steak sandwich, no onions, and fries." He turned back to Mercy, as soon as Steve was out of earshot. "Don't tell me you've become one of them?"

"One of what?"

"Those girls who only picks at her food in front of other people. You know you're already skinny, right?"

Embarrassment pushed through her veins, white-hot and leaving her skin burning. She couldn't keep the hurt from her voice. "I do know. Thanks for pointing it out, though." Okay, so she didn't have gorgeous curves like Liz, or the kind of voluptuous tits some of Andrew's starlets had, but it wasn't her fault. She had a high metabolism. And God damn it, if she didn't get enough grief for it from pretty much everyone ever, which included countless *advice sessions* from well-meaning teachers and colleagues, trying to get her to own up to eating disorders she didn't have.

Liz knew better, and Mercy thought by some stupid extension Ian would remember how much the teasing bothered her when they were younger. That was a mistake on her part.

"I didn't mean anything by it." Was that actually apology in his eyes? "A joke gone wrong. I'm sorry. If you weren't hungry, you should have said so."

She wouldn't meet his gaze. Refused to see any pity in his eyes. "Maybe I liked the excuse to spend some more time with—" She snapped her jaw shut before she could say more. There was no reason to whine about this or toss it back in his face. "Forget it."

"I'm sorry. It was thoughtless of me." He reached across the table and trailed his finger over her knuckles.

He wasn't supposed to sound sincere. Why was he being so irritatingly… *scripted* tonight? "It's all right," she said. "Or rather, it's not, but the apology helps."

And now the conversation was over. So much for shifting things back toward sexy and playful. The sum total of zero topics for changing the subject flew to mind. She could ask him about Marx. That was what started it back in the day. Or tease him about selling his soul to *The Man*, to run Thompson advertising—a joke that might fall as flat as his did.

The food arrived, and still they didn't do more than exchange bland nods and mumbles. She poked at her soup, even less hungry than before but feeling compelled to eat it anyway.

"Most interesting advertising request you've ever gotten?" Ian's tone was neutral, and the question drew Mercy's attention. "I'm not looking for details or names. I just like a good story."

This was a conversation she didn't mind. "Well… Despite the nature of my clients, I'll be honest of their requests are pretty basic and straightforward. Their ads have to be search-engine friendly, depending on where we place them, so the most creative it gets is finding new ways to say, *hot naked people for all your fetishes.*"

"For some reason, I pictured a lifestyle of hot-tub parties and ecstasy-laced margaritas."

"No you didn't." She wasn't sure how she knew he was teasing. His voice didn't give it away. There was the faintest smile around his eyes, and she only recognized that because Liz got the same look when she thought she was being clever and didn't want to let on. This was so much better than dancing around Mercy's insecurities—or stabbing them in the eye with a pointy stick, as the case may be. "I bet, Mr. I-have-expense-accounts-from-here-to-Timbuktu, your stories are way better than mine." His comment about her weight still stung, but pushing forward made it easier to mute the nagging in her head.

"Not really. Though there is the occasional hot-tub party." He talked between tiny bites of his food and never mentioned she only picked at hers.

"No? Nothing in all your vast experience has stood out as bizarre?"

"There are always little things."

An impish impulse snaked through her, and she reached across the table, to steal one of his fries and dip it in her soup. "Like what?"

"We had a guy once, who wanted an infomercial. You know—half-hour spot, late-night TV, to hawk his wares."

"People still make those?"

"Yes." Ian laughed. "Some of us still live in the Stone Age and don't know much about things like crowd funding and YouTube. Anyway, he insisted this product of his was amazing. Socks, gloves, various braces, that would pull the impurities from the body."

"As in, chemical toxins and such?" It didn't sound like such a unique idea to her. But there was always a catch.

"As in, the multitude of evil spirits that inhabit each person."

She almost choked on her bisque. "You're serious."

"He certainly was."

"God." Possibilities bounded to life in her head. "I can just picture this thing. *But wait—there's more. Act now, and we'll throw in the vinyl summoning circle, so you can control your own exorcised armies.*"

"They'll clean your dishes," Ian joined in. "Scrub your bathrooms. They even do windows."

The commercial practically wrote itself. "And for today's low introductory price of just nineteen-ninety-nine, we'll throw in a second set of Exor-socks in beige. That's right. Two pairs for the price of one. Rent your extra minions to the neighbors."

They both dissolved into fits of laughter, which died and revived each time one of them tacked another offer onto the end.

When she caught her breath, Mercy asked, "So what happened to him?"

"He insisted no budget was too big, so we mocked up a script and proposal, and sat him down. Nothing this good, mind you, but it wasn't bad." Ian shoved his half-finished sandwich aside and leaned in, fingers intertwined. "We gave him a rough estimate on price, and he balked. Said he wasn't paying more than five-hundred dollars, and we were a bunch of crooks."

"It takes all kinds." The restaurant had emptied while they talked, leaving them alone in the back corner. How long before someone started hinting it was time for them to leave? She wasn't quite ready for that.

Mercy heard Steve's *oh, shit* seconds before something light struck her shoulder, and wine spilled down her front, soaking her in red.

Chapter Four

"Jesus. I'm so sorry." Steve was by her side in an instant, handing her a towel and reaching for napkins.

She waved him away. "I got it." The last thing she needed was this kid dabbing a house red from her boobs... which were rapidly cooling, nipples drawing to hard nubs.

"I'm so sorry. I'll get more towels."

"It's okay." She stopped him. "I'll clean up in the restroom." Steve scampered off, and Mercy looked up to find Ian watching her, his gaze drifting between her chest and face, and a half-smile playing on his lips. "Enjoying the show?" she asked, his attention chasing away any irritation about being spilled on.

"It's a good look for you." Laughter tinged his words. "Do you want help, cleaning up? I can make sure you get all rinsed off and patted dry."

She was tempted to take him up on the offer. "Thanks, but no. I'll be back in a few minutes." She almost looked over her shoulder, to see if he was watching her walk away, but a tiny voice told her she didn't want to know.

A couple dozen paper towels later, with the assistance of generous helpings of soap and water, her sweater had a faint burgundy hue to it, instead of looking like she'd been stabbed. It still clung to her skin, damp and wrinkled. Her night was probably over.

When she approached their table again, Ian stood. "That top looks like it's seen better days."

"And just as many bad ones." She couldn't find enough annoyance in her, to be pissed off. The night was pleasant, despite its bumps.

He shrugged out of his jacket. "Turn around."

"I— Why?"

"You need this more than I do." He stepped behind her and pulled the suit jacket up her arms and onto her shoulders.

She should argue. Tell him she was fine. As the faint scent of his cologne washed over her, and his lingering heat sank into her skin, she decided obligatory protests could wait their turn. "Thank you."

He rested a hand at the small of her back—God, that felt good—and pointed her toward the door. "Do you want to get out of here?" he asked. "The manager stopped by and apologized. Comped the meal. Insisted you bill him for the top."

"That was nice of him. It was an accident."

"I know. I left the kid a good tip, though you should still charge them for the sweater."

"I picked it up for two bucks in Peru. It's time I retire it." She wasn't sure what else to say. They made their way back to the parking lot. As they approached Ian's car, she turned to him, to thank him for the evening. Her words died in her throat when she realized how close he stood, face inches from hers.

He adjusted the lapels on the jacket, tugging it closer around her, and trailed his fingers down the front. His hands drifted centimeters from her skin. If she thrust out her chest, he'd brush her nipples. So, *so* tempting.

"You look good in this." His tone was low and husky, and his gaze traveled the same path as his hands.

Not as good as you do. Again, her voice failed her.

He stepped closer, boxing her against the car. "I desperately want to kiss you, Mercy. And I'm praying you'll tell me *yes*."

She forced her vocal chords to work. "Yes."

He brushed his lips over hers, and a moan slid from her chest. When he deepened the kiss, gliding his tongue into her mouth to wrestle with hers, she groaned. The rough, damp fabric of her sweater bit the rigid peaks on her chest when she pressed into him, and an ache of need grew between her legs. She wanted more of this. More of him. A bit of groping in the parking lot wasn't going to sate the throb pulsing through her.

He rested a hand at the base of her neck, palm snuggled against her jaw, and held her captive. He caught her bottom lip between his teeth, before letting go and pulling away. "Fuck, you're a challenge."

She wasn't sure how to take that, but she liked the sound of it. "It's not as delicious if you don't have to work for it."

"That's exactly what I mean." He nudged her head back and drew his mouth up the side of her neck. "You're carrying on half of an intelligent conversation"—his lips vibrated against her skin—"while I'm trying to keep up and not sound like a moron." He pressed into her, and his erection dug into her stomach, teasing and tempting. "And all my blood's already rushed to a different extremity."

Why did they leave the hotel? She couldn't remember now. At least they'd parked in a back corner of the lot, and no one else was around. "I'm not letting you strip me down out here any more than I would have back there." If he called her bluff, he'd find out she was pretty willing either place. Excitement danced along her skin, and the way his jacket embraced her was intoxicating.

He settled his other hand on her stomach, and the heat of his palm scorched away the chill from her damp top. "I can do a lot without taking off your clothes." He inched higher as he talked. When he dragged his thumb across her rock-hard nipple, she whimpered. "And don't think for a minute I didn't notice you're not wearing a bra," he said.

"What did you have in mind?" Her question was punctuated by gasps for breath. He abraded the swollen nub, and she rocked her hips in time to his attentions.

"Nothing specific. More of an overall desire to make you come, and watch you pant and squirm until then."

She heard enough dirty talk in her line of work, most of it came off as cheesy and forced. Something about the way he spoke drove straight to her core.

Maybe it was because he meant it, or simply that the way he fondled her, pinching and twisting at the right time, flooded her thoughts with temptation and promise. "I'm good with playing things by ear," she said.

"And they are adorable ears." He traced his tongue along the curve of one, before nibbling and sucking on the lobe.

She almost didn't believe this. Ian Thompson, the biggest crush she had growing up, was feeling her up in a dark parking lot. Because he wanted to. She should get some kind of achievement-unlocked trophy for this. On top of everything else, he'd found almost every erogenous zone she had above the shoulders. He bit into her shoulder, playfully at first, and increased the pressure when she groaned. Correction—he'd found them all.

She dug her fingers into his arms, to steady herself, and her hips moved with a mind of their own, gyrating with each new pinch, tug, or lick from him. It was all incredible, but it wasn't going to get her off.

He dragged his palm down her stomach and inched under the waistband of her jeans. He'd either read her mind or her desperate grind gave her away. She didn't care which, as long as it worked. When he parted her folds and brushed her clit, she jerked against his hand.

"Good spot?" His laugh was strained.

"Perfect spot."

He traced circles around her sex. When she cupped him through his slacks, he increased his pace. She stroked his erection as best she could but lost track of everything as he pushed her closer to the edge. Her thoughts fuzzed, and pleasure spilled through her. She bit the inside of her lip, to keep from screaming into the night, intensely aware they were still in public—and more than a little turned on by the fact they might get caught. That wasn't supposed to make her hotter.

He zeroed in on the right spot, and she whimpered louder. "Right there," she managed.

He picked up the speed but didn't change the pressure, and orgasm built inside, nudging, pushing her toward the edge and then over. She gripped his arm tighter when she came, digging her nails through fabric and into skin. Scrambling for purchase. She rasped against his touch, until it was too much and her body shuddered away.

"You're gorgeous when you come." He laid kisses along her jaw, up her cheek, and finally on her forehead.

She managed a chuckle and sagged against him. "You're biased."

"Maybe. But I'm pretty sure I know what I'm talking about."

She extracted his hand from her jeans and held his gaze when she raised his fingers to her mouth. One at a time, she licked them clean, trailing her tongue along each pad, and spending several seconds on each tip and knuckle.

A low growl rumbled from him. "That's not fair."

"Why not?" She dragged his last finger over her bottom lip, pulling out a pout before letting go of his wrist.

"Because"—he pressed into her, erection hard and insistent against her stomach—"you said I couldn't strip you down out here, and I'm already struggling to keep that in mind."

*

Mercy scrunched up her face and wrinkled her nose in thought. "And you said, *I can do a lot without taking off your clothes.*"

When she reached for his belt and bent her knees, Ian had to draw on the last of his willpower, to grab her and pull her upright. She was willing to give him a blowjob, without prompting. Yet he preferred to drop her off and keep the memories of the night as they stood, rather than let her do something she'd regret if they got caught. What the hell was wrong with him?

"You don't have to do that." He couldn't help stealing another kiss. "I'll take you back."

"I suppose." She didn't argue. Damn, why didn't she argue? Instead, she stepped aside, let him open the door, and slid into her seat.

He adjusted himself as he strode to his side of the car. This was going to be the longest drive in history, and after he dropped her off, he still had another half hour up the canyon before he got home. When he was seated, he realized she was kneeling on the seat, watching him, a deceptively innocent smirk dancing on her full lips.

"What are you up to, Mercy?" His throat was dry from need. He wished he could fuck her right now. The seats in the back folded down, and the thing had tinted windows. His resolve not to push things was rapidly evaporating.

She dragged a single finger along the bulge in his slacks, teasing his cock, tracing over the head and back down the other side, before she reached for his zipper. "Returning the favor."

And… his resistance was gone. He didn't care they sat in a public place. No one was around, anyway. The only thing he could focus on was her cool, soft skin when she freed his shaft. She ran her tongue over the tip of his cock, and he leaned his head back with a groan. She took his length in her mouth, and he couldn't help tangling his fingers in her hair.

The tug seemed to spur her on. She moaned, and the vibrations traveled through his skin. He was already aroused. Her steady pumping and her lips gliding along his length propelled him toward climax. He didn't want to come though. Not yet. This felt too good. When she caressed his sac, his balls tightened and every muscle in his body coiled taut and on alert. He struggled to hold back. To focus on how good her mouth felt, without falling into climax.

It wasn't working. "I can't. I'm too close."

"Good." She managed between licks. She looked up, wide eyes meeting his. "I want to taste you."

Something inside him snapped, as if her words cut the spring holding him in check. He tightened his grip, and she whimpered but didn't slow down. Like a gale rushing through him, his veins burned over every inch of his body, and he clenched his jaw. He spurted against the back of her throat, drowning in the sensations. Losing himself in her scent, the delicious sounds she made—all of it. He pounded until he was spent, and then sank back.

She trailed her tongue along his skin, and he shuddered at the coarse texture on hyper-sensitive flesh. He pulled her up and crushed his mouth to hers, hungry and desperate to be close a fraction longer. She finally broke away and fell into her own seat, a light giggle flitting from her. It was such an amazing, carefree sound. He reached over and intertwined his fingers with hers, focused on even breaths, to bring his pulse under control and stop the shaking in his legs.

Neither one of them spoke for several minutes.

"I should get back." She broke the silence. "I kind of don't—" She shook her head. "Yeah, I should get back."

It made sense. The night was over. They'd both gotten a taste of what they wanted.

"Sure." He couldn't find any other words and refused to think long enough to grasp them. Thinking meant accessing ideas he wasn't ready to examine.

They drove without speaking, and she didn't let go of his hand until they neared her destination, except to let him shift.

The moment he stopped in front of the hotel, she hopped from the SUV. In his jacket. Not that he cared. He'd enjoy the view while she strode inside, and the memories of tonight were a fair price to pay for a replaceable piece of clothing. Instead of walking away, she circled the car—legs elongated by the headlights—stopped next to his door, and tapped on the window. When he rolled it down, she leaned in and settled her arms on the edge. Fuck, this woman knew how to show off her assets.

"Thank you for tonight." A hint of hesitation lined her words. Some of her bravado had evaporated.

He rested one hand on her cheek and kissed her again, burning the sensation of her soft lips into his mind. "The pleasure was all mine."

Even in the dim lighting, he saw the flush on her cheeks when she pulled away. That was new. And as enthralling of the rest of her. She shrugged out of his coat and handed it over. "See you again in twelve years."

"Yeah. See you then." His words faded as he watched her head inside, never looking back at him. A few seconds later, the reflection on the glass stole her from view. It was a good thing they were going their separate ways. Mercy wasn't an addiction he wanted to form. There was too much past and too much obligation there. Breaking off something hot and heavy with her further down the road—and it would end badly; relationships always did—would hurt Liz too. It would force his sister to choose sides.

Nope. He wasn't doing that. Twelve years was a good span of time for him to keep his distance.

Chapter Five

Mercy groaned and rubbed her eyes, but the exhaustion didn't ebb. A tiny lapse in memory on her part, and now it was barely nine in the morning, and she was sitting on a hotel couch, trying to wake up. How had she forgotten Liz was a morning person?

"I already showered, so you can get in there right away." Liz chattered away, as if it were normal for someone to be chipper and alert before the sun was awake. She didn't even have the decency to have a hangover. "Check in at the other place isn't until noon, but I thought we'd get breakfast first, and I wanted to give you time to change your flight if you need to."

At least Liz sounded happier than last night. It had Mercy a little worried. There should be more grief and mourning. That would come later, she supposed. "Wait. Flight changes?"

Liz poked her head back into the living room. "We're going on a honeymoon, remember? Ten days of debauchery?" Liz's chin quivered for the briefest of seconds, and then a plastic smile slid back in.

"You were serious about that?" Mercy extracted herself from the blankets twisted around her. As consciousness swept in, so did the night before. Her ruined sweater. The conversation. After. Holy shit, what came after. It was only a one-time thing, she had no desire for more, but damn, that was one hell of a memory.

"Come on, sleepyhead. Clock's ticking." Liz handed her a cup of coffee.

It came from the in-room maker, and it was basic, but Mercy was pretty sure it was still an elixir of the gods. She took a couple sips, not caring it scalded her tongue, then gathered her clothes and headed into the bathroom. She emerged sometime later, feeling much more prepared to face the day. She ran a list of to-dos through her head. What she could accomplish from her phone, on the drive to the hotel, and what would wait until after. She grabbed the phone next to the couch and called the front desk, to let them know she was checking out early.

They read back the last four numbers of the billing card on file, and her brain stalled. "I'm sorry. Say that again?" she asked.

"The card is for Thompson Advertising. It was changed out last night."

Ian. Warmth snaked through her. He did that for her?

"You all right?" Liz's question broke Mercy's rambling thoughts. "You look like someone punched you in the gut."

He did it because his sister was staying here. Disappointment and embarrassment pushed everything else aside, and pride joined it. "I didn't authorize that." Mercy could almost hear her credit card weeping, as she spoke. "Change it back to the original card please."

"We can do that for the room, but your assistant was emphatic that the ancillary charges be taken care of *right now*. Those have already gone on the new card."

The room service. "I see. Thank you."

"Mercy?" Liz snapped her fingers. "You all right?"

"Just shaking off some side effects." Of the pack Alpha taking care of his sister cub. Something twinged in Mercy's chest. If she gave it any attention, she'd say it was a whisper, wondering what it would be like to have someone watching her back that way and her returning the favor. Fortunately, she wasn't giving it any attention.

Liz studied her. "You're not hung over, are you? You barely drank anything."

"I'm great." Mercy almost believed her own smile. If she kept it on long enough, it would become truth. "And ready to go if you are."

A few minutes later, Liz's car was packed, Mercy's was returned to the rental place, and they were headed toward the mountains.

Liz plugged her phone into the aux jack, and an upbeat dance remix pumped from the speakers. If Mercy shoved aside the train-wreck of the last twenty-four hours and the amazingly explosive conclusion, this felt like old times. She and Liz filling the gas tank, pointing one of their cars in a direction, and seeing what nifty little hidden spots they hadn't discovered yet in Utah.

"What did you two get up to last night, after I fell asleep?" Liz's question caught Mercy off-guard.

The images that teased her all morning flooded in, unrestrained. Being pressed against the car. Ian traveling his mouth along her neck. The things he did with his fingers. She mentally shook herself. "Us two, who? What makes you think I got up to anything?"

"Defensive much?" Liz's laugh was strained. "I woke up in the middle of the night, had to pee, saw your note…"

Mercy looked up, to see Liz watching her. "And?" Mercy asked, when Liz didn't continue.

"Oh, God. You slept with him, didn't you?"

"No. There was absolutely no sleeping involved. And both of us stayed fully clothed." Who knew that would come in handy for denial, later on? "Speaking of, did you return his calls? He said something about a lawyer and your stuff."

"I'll call him later. When I said we should spend the next week indulging in debauchery, I meant once we arrived there. And not with Ian. He's my brother, for Christ's sake."

Mercy tried to ignore Liz's implication, but it dug under her skin. Liz had never judged her before. Mercy had to be reading her words wrong. "So I'll spare you the details, and you can be grateful you didn't walk in on us."

"But… You can't hook up with him."

"Why not?" An edge crept into Mercy's question. "And why won't you call him back?"

"Because you don't take things like relationships seriously."

The words hurt more than Mercy expected. They were true, but she didn't like the way they sounded coming from Liz. "I don't know if you realize this, but neither does he." Lines like the ones he used last night; the smooth glide from conversation to seduction; the outright suggestion they take attachments off the table—Ian had done this before.

"Exactly," Liz said.

"What?"

"You're my two favorite people in the entire universe, and I want to see you both happy. If you're screwing each other, you're not available to find that one person who will show you love isn't a joke."

Like true love has done you so much good. The moment the words slammed into Mercy's head, her gut twisted with guilt. How cruel was she? Liz was being sweet, like Liz always was, and Mercy wouldn't throw that back in her face. "You're right. And it doesn't matter. It's not like it's going to happen again."

"Which is another reason not to call him. He doesn't need to know what we're up to. Let's go find us way cuter guys as distractions."

*

As soon as he was out of sight of the café entrance, Ian crumpled the waitress's number, along with the scribbled note—*Call me*—and tossed it in a nearby trashcan. Even though he put in the time to flirt with the curvy brunette, he wasn't in the mood for the effort it would take to follow through. Maybe it was getting up early enough for a 6 AM conference

45

call, or the two hours of yammering before he had his coffee. *She won't be as much fun as Mercy was.*

So what? Mercy was probably on her way back to Georgia by now.

Seeing her last night was a trip to the past, but not in a bad way. When Ian was sixteen and his family picked up and moved halfway across the country, Liz threw a fit. She was supposed to be starting high school in the fall. Moving here meant another year of Jr. High, and leaving all her friends behind. Then she met Mercy—the daughter of one of the agency's clients—and the two were instant best friends. Trauma forgotten.

For Ian, moving back then was the best thing that had happened to him up to that point. In Chicago, he was the nerdy kid, built well enough to go out for sports, but not interested in physical competition. He liked a mental challenge. He was on the chess team and in the computer club, and the only reason he didn't get beaten up more often was he fought back.

In Park City, he was the bad boy. The new kid the girls swooned over, who didn't go to church like everyone else and had the nerve to say why not. He and Mercy formed a bond too, but it wasn't the same as what she shared with Liz.

Ian fell into step with the light morning crowd, and headed toward the parking garages of downtown Park City.

"Two minutes. I need to call my art guy," Mercy's voice mingled with his meandering into the past and flung him back to the present.

He whirled to scan the sidewalk at the sound of her voice, then slapped himself mentally when he realized what he was doing. Great. Now he was hallucinating her. That was fucked up. His phone rang, and he grabbed for it, grateful for the distraction. "Yeah."

"How was the wedding? And the earlier-than-God-gets-up call?" It was his assistant, Jake. "I know you'll probably be in the office soon, but you'll want to hear this now."

"You don't want to know. And hear what?"

"KaleidoMation called while you were on with Boston. They've narrowed their choices down to two companies, and we're one of them."

This was the kind of news Ian needed. The account would be a step into a new market for them, pushing past the legacy media his mother and grandfather built the company on, and into modern technology. They'd done a bit of work here and there, but nothing as intensive as KaleidoMation wanted. "Fantastic news. You've got everyone working on next steps?"

"Yes." Jake sounded insulted by the question. "Two catches, though. They're concerned about our lack of experience with social media, and they'll be in town Thursday and Friday, to talk in person about how we're going to handle things. Your schedule's been set, and I've made travel arrangements for them."

Normally, Sales handled new accounts, but this client was significant enough, Ian was involved in negotiations from day one. It was too bad he couldn't bring Mercy in, to consult. The kind of experience she had—

How many times was he going to have to squash thoughts of her? This wasn't about last night, though. From what he'd seen and heard, the woman knew her stuff. And the reaction she had to him suggesting they work together meant she was keeping that knowledge to herself. "Thanks for the heads-up, and for being on this." Ian clicked off the locks on his SUV. "I'll be in the office in ten minutes. We'll talk details then."

He'd throw himself back into work, shake whatever funk had Mercy's face, body, and intoxicating moans haunting his thoughts, and land his company a huge success. Exactly the way it should be.

Chapter Six

Mercy angled her chair at the table in the back of the bar, so she could see the entire room. The place was too bright and clean to be cliché. It kind of squicked her out. A cute guy at the counter had smiled at her a couple of times, but she couldn't find the enthusiasm to return the interest. Liz was with someone else, laughing, twirling her hair around her finger, and with far fewer drinks in her than her behavior implied.

Liz got a text from Ian earlier, asking where she was and for her to call when she had a minute. She promptly ignored it. She was afraid if she talked to him, she'd let it slip they were in the honeymoon suite, and he'd try and talk her out of binging and indulging. Mercy didn't have a good argument against that. She'd told Liz what he wanted, his text confirmed it, the rest was between them.

Mercy and Liz spent the afternoon seeing the town, stepping into overpriced souvenir shops, and visiting the sprinkling of art galleries along Main Street. It was a pretty little town—Mercy could admit that, despite the memories it held. She could do without the proliferation of faux-wood facing on every single building. It didn't build atmosphere so much as make it look like the city was trying too hard.

Mercy tried to get into the tourism, but the email waiting for her kept nagging. The note from the client she'd been wooing, KaleidoMation, saying they'd narrowed their decision down to two choices, and they'd like her in their offices early next week, to talk about options. Their biggest concern was whether an agency the size of hers could handle their needs. She itched to get back, to work on a proposal proving she had what it took.

She took her phone from her purse, pulled up a note app, and scribbled thoughts. Now seemed like as good a time as any, while Liz was distracted, and Mercy couldn't find the motivation to blather with a stranger. Every few seconds, she looked up, keeping track of her surroundings.

A text came from Liz. *If I'm not back in 10, don't send help.*

Mercy glanced in her friend's direction and got a wave and smile from Liz, before she and her companion wandered off toward some dark corner. Mercy shook her head and turned back to work.

Seconds turned into minutes, and she lost herself in her ideas. The ideas flowed. KaleidoMation picked her company to make it this far, she could address any of their concerns. She simply needed a killer presentation and the right reassurances that size didn't matter—it was how one used what they had. Sure, everyone said it, but recognition and relating to the consumer was important in this business.

The nearby scraping of chair legs across hardwood jarred her from her work, and she jerked up her head to see Cute Guy taking the seat across from her. Except he wasn't quite so cute up close. There was a hesitation in his smile. A lack of confidence Ian didn't suffer from.

As soon as the name entered her thoughts, she snarled at herself. Of course he wasn't Ian. That was last night. It was time to move on.

"You look bored over here in your corner." He scooted his seat closer. "Head down. Tweeting your friends. Someone might think you don't want company."

The assumption made her grind her teeth. "*Someone* might be right."

"Don't be like that, doll." Another scoot of his chair, then one more, and she was pinned between him and the wall. "You wouldn't be here if you weren't looking for something," he said.

On another night, in another town, she'd be in the bar because she wanted to get laid. She'd fall into the aggressive blandness. Not with this guy. He'd set her alarms off, even if she were in the mood. "I *am* looking for something. How did you know?"

"I'm psychic." He glided a hand up the inside her leg.

She jerked away and stood in a single motion, relief sliding in when she saw Liz emerge from the back rooms. Her friend wore a bright smile that didn't reach her eyes. Apparently they were both off their game tonight. "Her." Mercy waved, to grab Liz's attention.

Mr. decidedly-less-cute-now, glanced over his shoulder, and his leer grew. "You kinky girl."

Mercy rolled her eyes. "Hey, gorgeous." She prayed Liz would play along. "The honeymoon suite awaits. You ready to get out of here?" She brushed past the creeper, not caring she jarred him with her shoulder.

"Hold on." He grabbed her wrist, fingers digging into skin hard enough to hurt. "There's room for all three of us."

Mercy ground her teeth together. "Let go of me, or I'll scream."

"Ooh, you're vocal, too. Filthy bitch. I've got something to cram in your mouth."

Liz sidled next to him and dropped her hand near his crotch.

"Your dirty whore girlfriend knows what I'm talking abou—" His eyes grew wide, and his jaw moved up and down, but no sound came out.

"That's my nail file." Liz's voice was low, but unwavering. "I jerk my hand up, and it probably goes through your balls. Kinky enough for you?"

The guy let go of Mercy's arm and shoved her aside. "Uptight cunt."

Mercy tried to keep her composure as she joined Liz. She took her friend's hand and glanced over her shoulder several times, as they made their way outside. They'd parked on the street, so there was no need to worry about the creeper stalking them in a dark parking lot. Acid and adrenaline churned in Mercy's gut, as they pulled away from the curb. Mercy was in the driver's seat, since she hadn't been drinking. She tried to find something to say. Anything. The best she managed was a *thank you.*

She'd dealt with creepers before, and wasn't above kneeing someone wherever she could if it came to that. Why had she hesitated? Something was distracting her. She gripped the wheel so hard, she wondered if she might crack it.

The rest of the ride to the hotel was silent. Fortunately, the town was small enough it only took five minutes to get there. They made it up to their room, and the moment Mercy unlocked the door and pushed it open, Liz rushed past her. Seconds later, retching echoed from the bathroom.

Mercy took the couple extra seconds to latch shut every possible lock on the door, then joined Liz, grabbed some water, and waited.

Liz leaned her head against the wall. Red splotched her cheeks. "Thanks." She took the glass and rinsed her mouth. "I don't know if I should have done that. What would I do if he called my bluff? Not stab him. Crap, are you all right? You looked terrified."

Mercy sank to the floor next to her. She'd give the suite that—the bathroom was huge. "I don't know what he would have done. I'm glad you were there."

"Do you deal with that a lot?"

Mercy couldn't ignore the twinge the question brought with it. Liz didn't mean to imply anything, though. It was an innocent question, because Liz knew Mercy had a more active social life.

"I hope your night was better. You were beaming until you saw us," Mercy said.

"Yeah… No. The guy was all sorts of sweet, and we were making out in the hallway, and I couldn't do it. How does anyone do that? He understood, though. Gave me his number, in case I changed my mind. Are you sure you're okay?"

Mercy had a feeling Liz wouldn't go through with it. It was the big reason she didn't protest. Liz wasn't made for flings. "I'm a little high strung. Do you want ice cream?" The more Liz said, the further below zero Mercy's desire to linger on the events in the bar dropped. She was grateful Liz had stepped up, no question about it. So why Liz's words rub her wrong?

"I'm good with that. Maybe skip the debauchery the rest of the week, and ski instead?"

Mercy managed a weak smile. "You ski. I'll sit in the lounge, with Irish coffee and my laptop. Otherwise, yes."

*

"Always a pleasure. Enjoy the rest of your day." Ian shook the hotel manager's hand and left the man's office. That was another contract negotiation out of the way.

"No. I ordered the HD sample. Yes, I'm sure that's what I wanted."

Great. Two mornings in a row, he hallucinated Mercy's voice. And she sounded irritated, instead of seductive. He rounded the corner leading to the lobby, and ground to a stop when he saw her a few feet away, pacing and talking on the phone.

She widened her eyes when she met his gaze, and she said, "Right. Fix it," before dropping her phone into her purse. Her smile was nervous. This wasn't right. She almost appeared… guilty? She definitely looked incredible. Jeans, sweater, hair in a ponytail—she'd probably be irresistible in a burlap sack.

He approached with a smile. No reason to be anything other than friendly, though he'd prefer it if the images assaulting him—leading her to a dark corner, sliding his hands under her top, hearing her moan again—would take a break. "Funny running into you here."

"Not really." Her laugh stuttered. "I'm on vacation."

"You should have mentioned you'd be in town a few more days. I could have hooked you up." Or they could have hooked up. *No.* That was a one-time thing.

"I didn't know. Last minute decision, and all that."

She was hiding something, but he wasn't sure how to coax it out of her. The way her gaze flitted around the room, landing everywhere but on him, asking her directly wasn't the way to go. "Couldn't get enough of me?"

"It's not that. Liz…"

That made sense. "Gave you her room."

"*Yes.* Exactly. Because it was pre-paid, and she didn't want your gift to go to waste. That would be silly. I'm here completely alone."

The pieces clicked for him. He knew what she was holding back. "Mercy?"

"Hmm?"

"You're a horrible liar. Where's Liz?"

"Pro shop. Looking for a new ski suit."

He rubbed his face, but it didn't help reassemble his jumble of thoughts. "So she was grieving, and you let her wallow on the slopes instead of working to figure out the next steps in her life?"

Mercy's posture shifted in an instant, her spine going rigid, as she crossed her arms. "Yes."

"She was dumped at the altar." He couldn't believe they were having this conversation. "She may not be thinking straight. Did that occur to you?"

"Did it occur to you that she's an adult and can make her own decisions?"

A retort died in his throat. Maybe he was being a little overprotective, but he'd told Mercy why he was looking for Liz. Liz would know too, if she'd returned his calls yesterday. "The longer she waits to resolve this issue with George's wife holding her things hostage, the harder it's going to be to resolve it."

"*What?* You didn't think to mention that detail—oh, I don't know—two days ago?"

"I told you there were issues getting her belongings." How did he become the bad guy in this?

"And I told her why she needed to call you back. But holding her stuff hostage? You left that out."

"I figured I'd give her the rundown the next morning. I didn't expect her to screen my calls. Liz doesn't do impulsive. She was dealing with a lot."

"Like a brother who doesn't believe she can think for herself?"

"That's not true." Everything he said, she twisted back on him.

"You know what? I'm not playing the messenger on this." Mercy nodded at something behind him. "You two talk to each other."

Ian spun, to see Liz standing a few feet back, shopping bags on one arm and eyes wide.

She smiled. "Hey. Funny running into you here."

Chapter Seven

Mercy had faked her share of—well—everything in her life, but this was the worst imitation of working she'd ever done. She squirmed in the leather chair in the attorney's waiting room, and tried to find a position that didn't make her butt numb.

Liz disappeared into his office nearly two hours ago. Mercy had offered to make the drive down into Salt Lake with Liz, because what else was she going to do?

Besides work.

She squelched the bitter thought under a blanket of guilt. She wouldn't get more done back at the hotel than here. Despite the random thoughts, she was worried about Liz. When she called Ian's lawyer, they told her she needed to come in sooner rather than later.

It didn't help Mercy's mood any that Ian had texted her twice since they left the hotel, despite Liz's promise to let him know as soon as she was done. His most recent retort was, *She didn't call me back last time.*

Had he been this persistent and overbearing, growing up? Mercy reached into the past, snagging memories of life before Ian graduated high school.

Actually, before he hit his senior year, the three of them were all friends.

The two were her link to sanity when her mother died. Kept her going as her views shifted and her siblings pushed her away. She, Ian and Mercy would stay up late into the night, talking about anything and everything. She was grateful she still had that with Liz, on those rare occasions they both had time in their schedules for it.

The latch on the office door clicked, and Mercy jumped. Liz emerged with the attorney, shook his hand, and they both murmured in low voices.

She turned to Mercy. "I'm sorry that took so long." Her tone was too loud in the somber room. "Are you all right? We should go. Are you hungry? I am. We shouldn't have skipped breakfast."

Mercy followed her to the car. "I could eat. Call your brother."

"Was he a pest? I'm so sorry. I swear I don't know what his problem is lately." Liz kept up a steady stream of short-sentence chatter, as she unlocked her car and slid into the driver's seat. "Give me a sec." She talked as she typed something on her phone. "There. He's all set. The lawyer said there might be snow tomorrow. It doesn't look like snow, though." She pulled onto the road.

Mercy wanted to force her to take a breath, but every time she opened her mouth, Liz kept talking.

"I want to hit up The Gateway tomorrow. They said it's going to take time to work things out with George's wife, to get my things back. Which sucks, you know? Let's come back down here and shop."

Mercy realized Liz had paused and was glancing between her and the road. Apparently, that required an answer. "I have to work," Mercy said. "It sounds like fun, but I've got a deadline."

"I know you're the boss and all, but you're on vacation."

"No, you're on vacation." Mercy struggled to keep the irritation from her voice. She *had* agreed to stay, but with a caveat. "I'm along for the ride, but I have things that require my attention."

Liz frowned. "I'll go by myself."

Mercy nudged her arm. "I'm sorry. I'd really like to go. Will you be okay?"

"I'm fine." The babble vanished in the clipped words.

"I know what happened hurts—"

"You *don't* know." Liz's retort bit, jagged and uneven. "You have no idea. You should, by this point in your life. But you don't."

Mercy's sympathy wavered, sliced by the sharp words, and she struggled for a neutral response.

Liz shook her head. "I'm sorry. That's not my point. I don't appreciate you patronizing me. You're supposed to be my friend."

"You don't like it?" Mercy didn't try and hold back her irritation. "You're right. I can't imagine what you're going through—now, or the first time your life was cruelly challenged. I don't have a fucking clue. I do know that, if you don't like your life, you change it. Not everyone has that option. You do."

"Change it, how?"

"I'm not you, am I? I don't understand what you're going through. You figure it out."

Liz gripped the steering wheel tight and pursed her lips. "That's not what I meant."

"It is." Mercy shouldn't have snapped. Should have been more sympathetic. But she couldn't find it in her to apologize. "Don't worry about it." She did soften her tone. "The answers are there, and you'll find them. I'm not saying that to be patronizing. You can do this—whatever it is—if you want."

"I guess."

"I'm here to listen," Mercy said. "To bounce ideas off. But the decision has to be yours."

The remainder of the car ride passed in silence. Liz's words still stung, eating away at Mercy. Maybe in the time they lived apart, though they kept in touch, they'd changed more than she thought. Would their friendship survive something like this? The severe thought caught her off guard. Of course it would.

When they got back to the hotel, Liz muttered she was going to hit the slopes, and Mercy took the excuse to grab her laptop and escape, under the premise of getting some work done. She wasn't interested in sitting in the hotel lobby and having a blank wall as background decoration. Fifteen minutes later, she'd snagged a hotel shuttle to downtown. There was a cozy little café she saw yesterday, when she was here with Liz. She'd get a table there, with a window seat, and tap out some work-type stuff.

First she had a phone call to make, and she'd rather not irritate the other patrons with her chatter.

She adjusted her laptop bag on her shoulder, fell into step with the foot traffic, and dialed Andrew.

"Hey, sexy lady." His greeting was chipper and drew her smile out without effort. "You sending me any good pictures?"

"Not of me. I got some gorgeous shots of an orange cat, when I was in New Orleans. Couldn't get her to sign a release, though."

His exaggerated sigh rocked the line. "You're being literal."

"I am. Adorable tabby. You would have loved her."

"You kill me, babe. What's up?"

Talking to Andrew helped sap some of the tension that had built over the past few days. It was the biggest reason they traveled together for so long. The teasing was fun, and even when it hopped a line into flirting, they didn't have any chemistry. They'd slept together a couple of times, years ago. Didn't click. They were both fine with taking things back to platonic after that.

"I'm working on a new account, and I need to bounce some ideas off you. Do you have time?" she said.

"Always, for you. Do I get pictures after we're done?

Her mood improved another notch. She'd have to find something while she was out, to bring Liz as a peace offering. "Of the orange tabby? As long as they're for personal use only."

"You're too good to me." He laughed. "Bounce away."

Ian signed the credit-card receipt for lunch and handed it back to their waiter. Normally he didn't mind an excuse to take a long lunch for business—chat with the clients, catch up, polish his observation skills.

Today's company was one of the few exceptions. When he took over the agency after his parents died, he'd done a huge overall on staffing. Focused a lot of his hiring on psychology majors, instead of sales. Wanted to get into how their clients thought.

He hadn't had the same flexibility with clients as he did with employees. Dean Rice, Mercy's father, was one of his least favorite. Today, dislike was amplified by the fact Ian was already struggling to get Mercy out of his head, and seeing Dean kept her there for the wrong reasons.

Everyone exchanged random small talk, as the group headed toward the exit.

Dean stepped up next to Ian. "I heard about Elizabeth's fiancé from friends. Or, I assume, her ex at this point. My condolences. I hope your sister is coping."

Ian gave him a tight smile. "She's doing fine, all things considered."

"And how's Melissa?"

Ian choked on the urge to grit his teeth. He kept his expression neutral and pleasant. "I'd rather not discuss personal matters at lunch. You understand."

He knew from multiple sources that when Mercy left home at eighteen and changed her last name, her father disowned her. Dean never talked about her, except in vague terms, and rarely by name. He'd been disgusted when Mercy's business started to grow, especially when he learned what she was advertising.

"I do." Dean paused outside and turned to shake Ian's hand. "As always, a pleasure meeting with…"

Ian mentally stalled, waiting for Dean to finish the thought. Instead, he heard a soft, "Dad?" behind him.

"Melissa." Dean stepped around him, and Ian whirled to see Mercy standing a few feet away, laptop bag slung over her shoulder, and expression frozen.

His building irritation from lunch coiled and twisted in with frustration. This was the Mercy he knew as a teenager. Intimidated. Uncertain.

"I didn't think you'd stick around once the wedding was over. Don't you have someone waiting to buy you?" Dean didn't approach her, and she didn't look inclined to move, either.

"I'm not a whore." She forced the words through clenched teeth.

"You talk like one."

And it was time to shut this down. Ian walked past Dean. "She's my two o'clock. Enjoy the rest of your afternoon, Dean." He extended his hand in greeting, as he approached Mercy. He held Mercy's gaze, never looking back and refusing to give Dean a chance to interrupt. "Thank you for making time for me, while you're in town. I know your schedule is busy."

He expected her to return the handshake, but her tight grip and the shock of heat that spilled through him at the contact caught him off-guard. She felt as if she was holding on for dear life.

A whisper in the back of his thoughts said he needed to let go soon, to keep this exchange looking natural. The blood pounding in his ears made it difficult to hear even that internal voice.

She stepped closer, rose on her toes, and dipped her head toward his. This was the part where he needed to break contact or he'd destroy the illusion of what was already a weak excuse. It didn't matter. Dean Rice could fire him, for all he cared.

Her hot breath fell across his ear, drawing more of his senses to life. "He's gone," she whispered. "Thank you."

This was better than a stolen kiss in the middle of the sidewalk. Ian stepped back enough to look her in the eye. "Always."

She hugged herself and moved out of the flow of traffic, to lean her back against the wall. "I should have realized he'd still be a client, but I never put a lot of thought into it."

"You know how these things work. Old money pays into old money. Have to keep the legacy alive." Ian took a spot next to her. Fading wood and chipped paint snagged at his suit coat, but it was replaceable. He watched people pass by, as he helped Mercy hold up the building.

"What happens when the legacy wants to be its own person?"

"Are you talking about me or you?" He glanced sideways at her.

A smile twitched on her face, almost breaking through her tension. "You tell me. Am I talking about you?"

Some days, he wondered. Scratch that—most days, he wondered. He took over the business, because it was what he was supposed to do. There were a lot of days he questioned his career choice, especially when he saw how people like Mercy did things. That wasn't a discussion he was prepared to have, with her or anyone. "Are you all right?"

"I'm okay now. Thanks for covering for me." She jammed her hands in her pockets, shifting her weight until her arm rested against his. It was so comfortable and casual. Something he hadn't done in years, but it felt right now. "I probably should have stood up for myself, but… You know," She said.

"Twelve years, no contact. You've had a hell of a week, and it's only Tuesday? Yeah, I know." He nodded at her laptop. "Are you getting any work done?"

"I got some in. But it's so gorgeous out here today, I thought I'd enjoy it."

And it was. Perfect ski weather. Powder on the slopes less than a week old, and bright sunshine melting the snow from every other place. "You didn't expect to collide with your past, though." For the second time, he wondered if he was talking about her or himself.

She leaned her head against his shoulder, before pulling away, taking two steps forward, and spinning to face him. "I never do."

Her haunted look had evaporated, replaced with bright eyes and cheeks pink from the cold. It wasn't the seduction he saw the other night. This was brighter. More innocent. And just as enticing. He shook the thought aside, but that didn't stop fire from racing through his veins with half-suppressed fantasies.

What were the odds they could hook up one more time, while she was in town? He wanted one more taste. Would she be interested?

Chapter Eight

It wasn't that Mercy's father was abusive. He *was* religiously conservative. Far end of the spectrum. She'd struggled through years of psychological torment in his house, when she realized her beliefs didn't match his. Her mother passed away when she was thirteen, and her father grew even more restrictive after.

Called her *stupid* when she asked about why he taught her certain things. Threatened her with damnation when she realized she wasn't happy with some of his rules. Told she could rot in hell for the rest of eternity, and he'd would bring the marshmallows, when she walked out of the house at eighteen.

She didn't hold any ill will toward her family. She got over that a long time ago. That didn't mean she was ready to face her dad, without a little advance warning and mental preparation. She owed Ian a lot, for stepping up when she froze, and for helping pull her out of her daze and into the bright day. It made it easier to shake off the gloom.

He stood across from her, back to the wall, one foot propped up, looking casual and out of place at the same time, in his suit.

"That's why I don't date local girls." He winked. "In a town this small, it means countless awkward encounters after we break up."

She could do this. Joking. Familiar territory. How was it possible after so much time? "If I remember right, you don't date local girls because they're uptight and only like sex if you promise them they'll still be virgins after."

He laughed. A rich sound that rolled over her skin and sank into her thoughts. "I managed to corrupt you," he said.

"I won't argue that for a second. But we weren't dating. Still aren't."

"Touché. Rub it in a little more."

"Not in public. Or at least not in the middle of the street." She stepped closer and raised her hand, tracing a finger along his chest.

He snagged her wrist, stopping her halfway, and searched her eyes, gaze shifting back and forth. "You've changed."

"Is that bad?" She didn't have any issues with what she'd become, but it would be a shame to cut things short if he did.

"So far, it's anything but."

She gave a playful tug and broke free of his grip. "I should let you get back to work. Thank you again for rescuing me."

"Always." How could a single word carry so much sincerity? "I'd say *see you around*, but I don't want to tempt fate into sending you home early. So enjoy the rest of your trip and try to give Liz a break?"

"I always try." It wasn't the mention of Liz that chipped away at her swelling good mood; it was that those were his parting words. But that was the way it should be. In a few days, she'd go back home, not see Ian again for ages—if ever—and find her next fling, account, and distraction.

The thought squeezed her chest, but she ignored the ache as she waved at Ian over her shoulder one last time and called for a shuttle back to the hotel.

* * * *

Several hours passed, and Mercy managed to find the headspace to dive into her looming presentation. Liz texted, to say she was night skiing, and Mercy decided the hotel lobby wasn't a bad place for work, after all. Less chance of running into anyone she didn't want to see than if she hit up Main Street again.

The sun set outside, the evening crowds rushed in and out, and she forced herself to keep her head down and focus on work. Doing anything else, letting her mind drift, brought her back to the conversation with Ian, and that was distracting. Something about it nagged in the back of her mind. It wasn't a bad feeling, but it frustrated her that she couldn't grasp it.

"Is this seat taken?" Ian's familiar voice cut through the noise in her head.

She didn't try to hide her smile. "If you're looking for Liz, she'll be on the slopes a while longer."

"I'll take that as a *no*." He dropped into the chair next to her. "I already talked to Liz. Did you manage to get any work done today?"

She nodded at her laptop. "That's what I'm doing now. What are you doing here?" The question came out wrong, with an anxiousness she didn't intend. She was grateful for the excuse to step outside her head, especially with him as part of the scenery, but he was a reminder of what had her thoughts in a mess.

"I'm looking for you."

The simple statement made her pulse skip a beat. "Why?"

He scooted his chair closer and rested his arms on the table. His heat radiated toward her, melting her muddled thoughts into one single pool of him. "I wanted to talk to you," he said.

Right. He was looking for her. She tried to tell her heart to stop pattering. That she didn't care. Her heart didn't listen. "You could have called."

"You're making this difficult."

"I don't know what *this* is. Fill me in, and I'll try to make it easier?"

He reached in his pocket and placed something on the table, hidden by his palm. It clanked against the wood with a light *ping*. "I heard a rumor you're on a tight deadline. I know hotel Wi-Fi isn't always the fastest or most secure, and roaming the streets in a town like this can be dangerous." He nudged a key toward her. "If you'd like to lock yourself away from everything tomorrow, my place will be empty."

Instinct told her to turn him down. He wouldn't be offering if he didn't want something. She hated that voice and that it chanted now, instead of letting her think of an appropriate response. "Thank you," she said, but didn't reach for the key.

"Can I ask what you're working on, or is that an insider secret?"

"You don't have to make conversation to fill the empty air." What was wrong with her tonight? Everything she said came out wrong.

He raised his brows. "Have I ever been a small talk kind of guy?"

The question triggered the memories from earlier. About their friendship, growing up. It also reminded her about her fight with Liz. Mercy decided to focus on the more pleasant aspects of the evening. "Maybe you've changed since I knew you."

"I have." He chuckled. "But not like that. I asked because I want to know. If you don't want to talk about it, tell me to fuck off."

Nope. He definitely hadn't changed like that. His genuine interest, the fact he wanted to talk to her—about her—warmed her from the inside out. Despite her reason insisting she was being silly, she liked the attention. "It's a really big client. I can't give you details; you know how that goes. It's the kind of account that, if I land it, our status changes from *struggling* to *almost making it*." As she spoke, his gaze never left her face. It wasn't the kind of attention she was used to. How wrong was that? "What?"

"Your eyes light up when you're excited about something. They turn a gorgeous shade of blue."

She wanted to lose herself in the compliment. To make all sorts of assumptions about what it meant.

They weren't going down that road. Unless it meant one more tumble—clothes off this time—before they parted ways for good. Talk about a distracting thought. "I should get back to work."

"I'm paying attention. I know you haven't said *yes*. Take advantage of the quiet tomorrow." He nudged the key a few inches closer to her.

"Because that's not awkward at all. Me, wandering around your empty house."

"If it makes you feel better, think of it as the family house. You know—the house you practically lived at?"

She did know, and she didn't have a good response.

"Don't turn me down because you feel like you're supposed to. We both know you'll get more done there," Ian said.

"What if that place holds bad memories for me?" she asked.

"Does it?"

She laughed. "Not even close. It'd be kind of nice to be back there. Can I ask why you're doing this?"

"I told you the other day—I have a lot of respect for what you do. Why's that so hard to believe?"

Because no one who said so meant it. Not people she slept with, anyway. They wanted sex, and they didn't care about what was inside the shell. She was fine with that. This whole I-like-you-as-a-person thing, from someone she'd screwed around with, messed with her head. Or maybe what weirded her out was that he seemed sincere and she wanted to believe him. When had she stopped taking people at face value? *When I got smart.* The answer made her wince internally; she didn't like facing her cynicism head on. She took the key. "I'll be there. Thank you."

And she'd pray her cynicism was wrong.

Chapter Nine

Ian did one last walkthrough of the office building, calling *hello* in each room and making sure the lights were out. Even though at least half his staff lived in the mountains, within a few miles, the two feet of fresh snow in the last couple of hours prompted him to send them home early. Those who lived in the valley left long before that, and he was grateful he'd shut down work for the day. The canyons were closing to any vehicles without chains or four-wheel drive.

He trudged to his SUV through the white, unable to keep it from soaking his slacks halfway up to his knees. Years of experience navigating the roads in weather like this made it no less treacherous. Too many people drove too slow or too fast. With the twisty, windy mountain roads, that got dangerous. He was glad Liz knew enough to stay in Salt Lake for the evening. She'd already told him she wouldn't be back tonight. One less thing to worry about.

He maneuvered his car along a route that should be familiar but looked foreign when it was covered in a white blanket. When he started sending employees home, he called Mercy. She didn't pick up, and he sent a text, asking her to let him or Liz know she was okay.

That was hours ago, and neither he nor Liz had heard back. Logic told him there was a rational explanation, but as he crept the vehicle along more slowly than he could walk, concern built inside. Liz dropped Mercy off at the house this morning, before she went down to Salt Lake. If Mercy wasn't at his place now, that would mean she called a cab, and Ian didn't trust any taxi driver, experienced or not, in this weather.

He still wasn't sure why he insisted Mercy work at his place today. On the surface, his reasons looked good. Mercy was on a deadline and those sucked. But underneath it all, he knew he wouldn't have made the offer to anyone else. He just couldn't figure out why.

Talking to Mercy yesterday, the way her face lit up and she almost glowed when he asked about work, almost made him forget it was a bad idea to ask her to join him in a back room somewhere. His cock had perked up for attention, and his brain argued that he was enjoying the conversation. He needed to get his head on straight, when it came to her.

Home was usually a fifteen-minute drive. Nearly forty-five minutes later, he pulled into his garage, gripping the steering wheel until the car was completely stopped. He lost track of how many cars around him slid in awkward directions along the way. Adrenaline thrummed hard and fast through his veins. He needed a drink. Neat.

The house was too quiet when he stepped inside. An odd thought, since it was always quiet, but he hoped Mercy was still here. Only because he needed to know she was safe. "Mercy?"

No answer.

He stripped off his coat and shoes and left them by the door leading to the garage. His suit jacket wound up draped over the back of a chair. He'd take it upstairs later. As he made his way to the liquor cabinet in the study, he strained his ears hard enough nothingness hummed back. And then another noise.

Was that keystrokes?

He paused in the study doorway and saw Mercy, head down and typing away. A tension he didn't realize was there evaporated from his neck. She sat half-turned toward him, focused on her laptop and wearing earbuds. It took him a moment to drag his gaze from her long, slender neck—exposed because she'd pulled her hair back—and the way her bottom lip caught between her teeth.

Time to stop staring. He had to shake himself. He knocked on the doorframe, and she still didn't look up. Temptation snaked through him—the desire to slide up behind her, tug on her ponytail, and drag his mouth along her neck.

This was his sister's best friend, and that was a relationship he couldn't breach. Liz had lost too much already. He strode across the room and stopped next to Mercy. When he placed a hand on her shoulder, she jumped and let out a little *eep.*

She plucked out her earbuds and slid her chair back. "I must have been more in the zone than I thought."

A laugh of relief slipped from him. "I'm glad you're all right."

"Why wouldn't I be? What do you know that I don't?" The light in her eyes and quirk of her lips said she was teasing.

"You weren't answering your phone. Speaking of—text Liz, tell her you're alive."

She glanced at the device next to her laptop. "Oh, that. I shut off my phone and told everyone in the office, if they needed me, it had to wait. I don't know if this place has some kind of magic mojo, but I haven't lost myself in work like this in ages. Thank you for that, by the way."

There was that gorgeous look again. The same one she had last night. Bright eyes, a hint of pink on her cheeks, and a lilt to her voice that made him think she was barely keeping a rein on whatever was in her thoughts.

"I'm glad you got something done," he said.

"It's only two." She glanced at her laptop. "Do you keep some kind of CEO, half-day hours?"

He nodded toward the balcony window behind her. From here, it was a view of the mountainside. On a clear day, anyway. Right now, it only showed clouds. He tugged her to her feet and let his touch linger, as he led her toward the sliding door. "Look outside."

"Oh. Wow." A cool blast hit them when she slid the glass open and stepped into the storm. "So much white." She only stood there for a moment before rushing back inside.

"The roads up from the valley are all closed, and most of the city is shutting down. Liz is staying in Salt Lake for the night."

"I should get back." Her gaze kept drifting toward the balcony.

"You may want to wait out the storm. The roads are a bit scary. I know; I was just on them, and the plows take their time getting up here."

"Even after all these years. I'm not surprised." She gave him her attention. The spark hadn't faded from her face. "Is that your excuse to keep me here?"

The hint of playfulness mingled with the adrenaline from his commute and flipped a switch on his thoughts. "I don't need excuses. I'm asking you outright. Stay."

"For my own safety. Right?"

This was too easy with her. Too much fun. "Not only for that, but mostly." It wasn't as if they were going to repeat the other night. Though, the way she licked her lips, his imagination leaped ahead to that possibility. This was spending an evening with an old friend. With his sister's friend. "Finish what you're working on or wrap it up, and then decide. If you spend the next forty-five minutes white-knuckling it, while the cab slips and slides along the hillside, you're not going to get anything done when you get to the hotel."

She glanced outside again, over her shoulder, concern whispering across her face. "That long?"

"That's how long it took me."

"So the Porsche isn't just your way of compensating? It serves a purpose?" There was no accusation in her light question.

"You tell me. Do I need to compensate?"

The way she traveled her gaze over him, from head to foot and back again, pushed his thoughts aside and left room for his nagging lust to surge to the surface. The corners of her mouth twitched. "I

don't think so. But I'm not the one who bought it."
The lights in the room dimmed, flashed back on, and
then went out completely, leaving the reflection off
the snow outside to illuminate the room. Mercy
furrowed her brows. "Laptops and battery power are
a lifesaver. You know?" She stepped around him,
then clicked a few things on her computer before
giving him her attention again. "Unless you have
backup power, I'm not getting any more work done
anyway."

"No backup. It doesn't really stay out long
enough to need one."

"Oh. So… I'll wait, then."

He grabbed her hand and tugged her toward the
couch at the far side of the room. "As long as you're
doing that, keep me company."

*

Mercy should have been more bothered by
having her afternoon of work interrupted. Instead,
she was grateful the power had been out for over an
hour and the roads stayed a wreck. It was an odd
sensation, the desire to spend more time with Ian, not
because he'd done amazing things with his fingers,
but because she wanted to catch up.

They'd moved into the living room, to be next
to the fireplace. Outside, the clouds blocked a setting
sun, but the reflection between snow and sky was
bright enough it spilled through the windows,
keeping the room from seeming too dark.

Ian wandered back in and settled next to her on
the sofa. He'd changed into jeans and a sweatshirt.

The first time she'd seen him in something casual this trip, and he still looked temping. His knee brushed hers, as he shifted sideways to see her. "The power company says ice took out the lines across most of the city. They don't have an ETA for when it will be back on. As much as I hate to say it, the resorts—like your hotel—will probably get power long before I do."

She gave him a pout and hoped it came off as teasing, despite the twinge inside "Are you trying to get rid of me?"

"Not even close. I'm trying to make sure you're comfortable. I can't even offer you dinner if you stay here."

"I make a mean PB and J." They'd spent their time flitting from one topic to the next, but nothing stuck. It wasn't the same easy banter they had the other night at dinner, and she didn't know how to find that mood. "And it's warm by the fire."

"Peanut butter and jelly, huh?" He trailed his finger on a lazy path along her leg. "Your domestic skills astound me."

She stuck out her tongue. "Don't knock the value of an incredible sandwich. I'm gifted at two things. Peanut butter sandwiches and blow jobs. Sometimes I wonder if I should have opened a daycare. All dads would want to drop their kids off." Even as the words slid out, she knew the joke was bad. A leftover she used, to keep people at arm's length. His frown said he felt the same. Why had she said that? Defensiveness kicked in. An old scar she couldn't ignore. "What?"

"You're worth more than that."

"It's a joke, Ian."

"It's a shitty one."

"Fine." Time to try yet another approach. "Let's play a game."

"I'll bite. What game?"

"Never Have I Ever." Everyone loved a good drinking game. Maybe she was too old for that, but a little alcohol would loosen them up, and they could get to know each other in the process. The rules were really easy. One person said something they'd never done, and if the other person had, the other person had to take a drink

"No."

There went that idea. "If you're worried about me emptying your liquor cabinet, I'll replace whatever we drink."

"Stop trying so hard."

The words dug deeper than she thought possible. "I don't know what you're talking about."

"I don't want you drunk. I don't want to play a game. I want to know more about you." His tone implied *more* went beyond superficial banter.

"Why?"

He draped his arm over the back of the couch and rested it against her shoulder. "Because the last few days have told me you're more fascinating than Liz realizes. More intriguing than the girl I used to know. I want to uncover that."

"You might say that now, but really you don't." There were those fucking scars again. The whispers telling her no man wanted more than what they saw on the surface. A trophy. Bragging rights. She was fine with that. It was when she let herself believe they *did* want more, that it hurt. "I'm really not that interesting."

He placed a finger under her chin and raised her face, to hold her gaze. "I'll be the judge of that."

She shouldn't read too much into his words—knew better than to fall into the illusion—but a glowing ember in her chest desperately wanted his interest to be sincere.

Chapter Ten

Twelve Years Ago

Ian shoved the last duffel bag into the trunk of his car. He was supposed to wait until morning, to pack up the last of his stuff, but it was almost 1 AM. He might as well do something useful with his insomnia.

He started when someone stepped from the shadows near the garage. "Fuck, Mercy. You scared me." He gave a quiet laugh.

She stood out of the light's reach. It was August, one of the few months when it was warm enough at night for shorts and a T-shirt. There were times he wished she were just a few years older. Closer to his almost-eighteen, instead of his sister's fifteen. Most of the time he was grateful it kept her off limits.

"I saw you moving around over here. I wanted to talk. Is that okay?" she said.

"Always." Well, until tomorrow morning. Then he'd be driving across state lines for college. "What's up?"

"You have to take me with you tomorrow. I have money for gas and enough to feed myself for a while. I've been saving up. I won't tell anyone. I'll be at the gas station. You can pick me up on your way out of town."

Shit. She'd given this some thought. He closed the distance between them, so he could keep his voice low. "I can't do that."

She furrowed her brow. "Why not?"

"Besides the whole *you're a minor and it would be kidnapping* aspect of the idea?"

"I can't stay here." A desperate edge crept into her whisper. "It's devouring me."

"You're being melodramatic." Despite his words, he felt bad for her. He couldn't imagine what it would be like to clash with his family the way she did with hers.

"And you don't have to put on a dress and be paraded around in front of your family's peers every Sunday morning."

He gave her a dry smile. "I've done my share."

"Please?" She grabbed his hand.

He kissed her on the forehead. "No. You've got this. Three years, and you'll be out of here, too." He pulled from her grasp and turned away.

"I hate you." Her words landed against his back.

"I'm sorry, Mercy."

"Fuck you. I hope college sucks."

*

Now

Ian wasn't sure what to make of the vibes rolling off Mercy. It was as if she was perched on a ledge and could be pushed in either direction with a single breath. He didn't like being uncertain about what to say next.

"We've talked a lot about me." Her tone was even and neutral. "I'd like to hear more about you. Why did you leave me behind?"

He didn't want to make light of that, but it seemed so long ago, and despite her reasons back then, the parting was childish. "You know why. Are you still upset?"

"Would you feel bad if I am?" Still no emotion reflected in her eyes. Her face was a blank mask.

"I've always felt bad, but I wouldn't do it differently."

Finally, the corners of her mouth tugged up, and a smile teased her eyes. "No. I'm not still upset. I hated you then, but I'm grateful now."

"I didn't expect that."

She shook her head, then leaned it against his arm, on the back of the couch. "I know it was awkward with my dad today, but while he summons the timid girl in me, sticking it out made me stronger once I left."

"Where did you go, anyway?"

"I noticed how quickly you turned this back on me." She shifted her weight, to lean better against the couch, and tucked her legs under her.

Even in the faint light bouncing through the windows, combined with the flicker of the fireplace, she looked amazing. Seeing her curled up and comfortable short-circuited his thoughts in a way he didn't expect. "I already know everything there is to know about me."

"Do you?"

"You do a lot of that—counter my questions with your own."

Her smile vanished, and her eyes went flat and dull. "Don't you?" A smirk, and then a laugh slipped out, before she finished her question. "I'm being weird. I don't know what's up with that." The weight of her head against his arm was warm and tempting.

"I like it." He adjusted his position enough, to trail his fingers through her hair. He wasn't sure where the impulse came from. Relief trickled inside, when she leaned into the gesture instead of pulling away. "Ask whatever you want, and we can talk about me," he said.

She scrunched up her face for a moment. "Are you happy with your job? Are you glad you took over the family business?"

"That's two questions." He didn't know why he was stalling. The answer was *yes*. Wasn't it?

"It's the same question. And it's the second time you've avoided answering it." She straightened in her seat. "I bummed around Europe and South America for a couple of years, then came back here, to work."

"And met Andrew Newton somewhere along the way." He didn't think his change of subject fooled her, but he didn't have an answer for himself, so he couldn't give her one. The uncertainty nagged him more than not being able to read her earlier. He always had an idea what was going on in his head.

"Yes. And I helped him market his porn site."

"I don't know." Ian hated those words. He never said them to anyone, even when they were true. He always had an answer.

Her expression softened, and she scooted closer, until her knees touched his leg. "Don't know if you like your work?"

"There are parts of it I like, but I'm not sure I'm happy I took over the company."

"So why did you do it?"

She had to go and ask the difficult questions. Then again, that had always been her. "What else was I going to do?"

"What you wanted, instead of what was expected of you." She fiddled with a loose thread on the tear in her jeans. "You taught me that."

"And you've never looked back?"

"Nope. Not really."

He dragged a finger along her arm. She closed her eyes and parted her lips in a tiny sigh. Images skipped through his mind. Leaning in, to press his lips to hers. Sliding his hands up her sides and stripping her shirt off in the process. Vivid and intense, they refused to be ignored.

He wanted to keep the conversation going, though. "What did you do after I left? The stuff you didn't tell Liz."

She met his gaze, an impish look on her face. "What makes you think I keep secrets from Liz?" Behind her, a log in the fireplace crackled as it split, and a flare of light danced through the room before dimming again.

He'd have to toss another one on soon. It was a good thing he'd refused to do the gas-powered replacement that required an electric switch. "Did you tell her you asked to go with me that night?"

Mercy shook her head. "Did you ever tell her how you… what were your words? Corrupted me?"

"I did say that, didn't I? No, I never told her you were the first person who listened to my ramblings about thinking for yourself and questioning authority, if needed, and shunning indoctrination. That shit got me kicked off the baseball team in Chicago, you know."

"I had no idea you played baseball in high school."

He tucked a strand of hair behind her ear. He wasn't sure where the intimate gestures came from, but they felt right, and she didn't seem to mind. "I didn't," he said. "I tried out and made the JV team. First day of practice, the coach got on my case for something… I don't remember what, now. I was wearing my socks wrong or something."

She shivered and rubbed her arms, drawing a frown from him. He hadn't realized how far the temperature had dropped. Nudging her to straighten, he pulled the throw from the back of the sofa. He prompted her to turn and tugged her into him. As she settled with her back to his chest, he pulled the throw over them both. "Better?" he asked.

"Much." She rested more of her weight against him.

The faint floral scent of her shampoo seeped into his thoughts and fuzzed them. He'd never liked cuddling, but this was comfortable.

She pulled one of his arms more tightly around her. "What did you say to him that got you kicked off? I'm assuming that's what happened."

Right. Ian was telling a story. He rewound the last several seconds of conversation, until he could think clearly enough to pick up where he left off. "I was reading a lot of Marx at the time—Karl, not Groucho."

"I figured." She giggled.

"So I went off on this long-winded rant, about how he was only a baseball coach because the bats made him feel like more of a man. How we weren't the subjects of some grand and mighty czar, and as collective, as a team, as a group who would be strongest if we supported each other, we should be allowed to wear our socks however we wanted."

"I'd have kicked you off the baseball team, too."

He rested his chin on her shoulder. "I think in the end, we were all happier that way."

Silence fell between them, punctuated by the crackle of the fire. Her steady breathing pressed against him, and he felt her heartbeat, slow and even, lulling him toward peace.

"I made friends." Her quiet words blended with the background noise. "Online, I mean. When I wasn't working or in school, I joined a butt-load of couch-surfing communities and made contacts all over the world. The day I graduated, I rented a cheap-ass motel room and stayed there long enough to have my name legally changed and get a new passport and ID. I took all five hundred dollars I'd saved, bought a ticket to Brazil, and played it by ear from there."

He knew part of this story. It wasn't a secret Mercy had bummed around the world. He'd never heard any details. Hadn't asked, and Liz never offered. "And you survived for the next three years on a couple hundred bucks." He couldn't keep the disbelief from his voice.

"No." She tilted her head back enough to look at him. "Sometimes I stayed on couches, sometimes I got cheap rooms. In between, I picked up work here and there. I washed dishes in Venezuela. I taught English in Portugal. And somewhere along the way, Andrew's sites started making money, and he paid me to make sure that trend continued."

"If I scan his archives, will I find pictures of you?"

She met his gaze. "Ian Thompson, are you asking if I ever did porn?"

"I guess technically I am." It wasn't what he meant to ask, but he was curious.

"He's got pictures of me, but I never signed the release."

A ping of jealousy rocked inside Ian, and he struggled to understand it. "I don't know if I'm disappointed or relieved."

"If you want to see me naked, you just have to ask." She stretched her arms over her head, grinding her ass into his hardening cock. Her sweater pulled up, leaving his hand resting on her stomach, and she didn't move to tug it back down when she was done.

"You're obviously not making that offer to everyone, or I'd be able to find those pictures."

"I'm not. But I yield for the right man."

The way she kept adjusting herself in his lap, added to the not-so-subtle teasing, had him rock hard. His mind was already tripping ahead, over different ways to strip her down. "So… we keep giving into these one-offs until the week is up, and then we go our separate ways?"

"*Keep giving in.* This is twice." She nudged his palm higher on her chest. "Yes, I'm keeping count. And yeah, that's how it works. Besides, the first time was really more like intense making out."

He chuckled. "I know. If you only put the tip in, it's not really sex."

"That's what the girls at church told me." Laughter danced in her words.

"I'm not stopping at the tip." He skated his thumb over her bare skin. "And if you tell me yes, I'm going to make sure you stay warm until morning—or until the power comes back on. Whichever comes last."

"I've always liked the way you think," she said with a gasp, arching her back when he bushed the bottom of her breast. The tiny sounds she made, combined with her faint scent and the weight of her body against his, plowed through his restraint.

He yanked her shirt over her head and trailed his mouth along the back of her neck. "And I'm intrigued that it's not easy to tell what you're thinking." He spoke against her skin.

He had a feeling this was going to be a night he remembered for a long time, even after she went back to her life on the other side of the country.

Chapter Eleven

Mercy closed her eyes and rested more of her weight against Ian. The sharp tang of burning wood filled her head and combined with the heat of his palms on her bare skin. He cupped her breasts, and she moaned in appreciation.

"If you ever want to know what I'm thinking, just ask." She gasped when he pinched her nipples.

"And you'll tell me?" He spoke between flicks of his tongue over her shoulder, along her spine, and at the base of her neck.

The chill on her face clashed with the warmth of the blanket, lighting up her nerves and flaring though her senses. It helped that, with each new tug and twist from Ian, she squirmed involuntarily, and his hard length dug into her ass.

"I might," she managed between grabs for air. "I guess it depends on what the question is." She arched her back when he dragged his finger across *that* spot that raced into her stomach, and continued between her legs, making her damp. "But your odds are a lot better than if you don't ask."

"What are you thinking now?" As he increased the pressure of his touch, the rest of her body ached for attention. Pleaded, each time she rubbed her thighs together. Begged, at the temptation of his erection pressing against her.

She adjusted her position and felt his cock jerk. The seam on her jeans dug into her slit, but it wasn't enough. "That you're a wicked, cruel tease."

"You think so?" He reached the spot on her neck where it met her shoulder, and sucked on the skin, drawing it in, scraping his teeth over it… marking her. At the same time, he tweaked harder, until the swollen nubs on her chest stung.

Lances of pleasure and pain rolled through her, and her moans grew louder. "I know so." She panted at the variety of sensations rolling over her. She'd had attentive lovers before. Also had her fair share of good, bad, selfish, generous, and virginal guys. The memory of those men paled compared to this, and she couldn't say why. He kissed the now-tender spot on her neck—his touch so faint, she wondered if she imagined it. Then again, she didn't want to devote the brainpower to her past. Ian was here, and she was going to dive into this for all it was worth.

"Stand up." He nudged her forward.

She did as prompted. The blanket fell away, and cool air grazed her hot nipples. The shock made her head swim. He laid the blanket on the floor near the fireplace and tugged her closer. His every caress was deliberate and confident. Everything felt simultaneously surreal and hyper-real, as if vivid fantasy shifted to reality, with Mercy caught in the middle.

Ian raked his fingers up her spine, over her neck, and caught them in her hair. When he crushed his mouth to hers, the clash of lips and dance of their tongues was demanding and desperate.

She needed to be closer. Wanted to melt into him. She tugged up the bottom of his sweatshirt, and he broke away long enough to jerk it off and toss it over the couch. When her cooling breasts pressed into his heated skin, it was like afternoon sunshine on fresh snow. A shock of brightness and warmth, colliding and melding with the elements.

He sucked her bottom lip between his teeth, before pulling away. "Fuck. You're a delicious temptation." Gravel undercut his words.

She was pretty sure he was sin wrapped in denim, with a dangerous mouth for a bow. She slid her hand lower and cupped him through his jeans. "So is this." Each time she stroked, his dick jerked against her hand.

"Lucky us, I've got that covered." He pulled a condom from his back pocket.

She raised her brows. "Do you keep a rubber in every pair of pants you own?"

"I haven't stopped fantasizing about you for more than a few minutes at a time since the other night." He unbuttoned her pants and pushed the rest of her clothes to the floor. His came off seconds later. "So yeah. I'm prepared." He cupped her ass and pulled her to him. Skin met skin, and desire danced in time with the flames. His cock pushed against her stomach. "Lie down."

He helped her lower to the ground, and then grabbed a pillow from the sofa, for under her head. She didn't know if she should beg to be fucked or for more teasing. Any more musings flitted away when he kissed down her chest and over her stomach, and drew his tongue up her slit.

His first licks were feather light, but he zeroed in quickly on her clit. She rocked against his face, focused on the rough texture against her swollen sex. He alternated between slow and fast, drawing her closer to the edge each time, but never pushing her over. When he drove two fingers inside her, she clenched involuntarily at the sudden intrusion. God. This felt incredible. She arched her back and tangled her fingers in his hair, holding him in place and letting orgasm build inside, until it broke past an invisible dam and spilled through her. She ground and writhed when she came, wanting more attention, but not sure how much contact her body could take before her nerves went on strike.

A series of shudders jerked her away from his touch, and he eased off. A pleasant haze circled her thoughts, fogging everything and granting a dreamlike quality to the sparking firelight. Her throat was raw. Had she screamed? She never got vocal during sex. Too many years sharing walls and rooms in hostels. She heard herself giggle, and the sound danced with the tear of foil.

Ian wedged her legs apart with his knee, supported himself on one arm, and brushed his mouth over hers. He tasted like sex and wood smoke. Her new favorite flavor. "I need to be inside you," he murmured against her lips.

She nodded, unsure where her voice had gone, but not motivated to find it. He dragged the head of his cock along her slit, from her opening to her clit.

With each pass, she squirmed from the overstimulation, but she didn't want to pull away.

"Problem is"—he nudged her entrance, pushing in enough to stretch her out before withdrawing again—"I'm rock hard, and the way you look and sound when you come is an aphrodisiac on its own. I'm not going to last long."

When he neared her opening again, she thrust her hips, driving him deep inside in a single push. "I don't care." Her words were raspy against her eardrums. She dragged her nails up his back and wrapped her legs around his waist. "I need to feel you."

His laugh was strained, and he held her gaze. His rhythm was slow. He plunged in to the hilt, then withdrew again almost completely before repeating.

She gripped his arms, sinking into the feeling. "Stop holding back." She forced the words through clenched teeth.

He slammed inside her hard, and again, building to a rapid pace. His face in this light was stunning. Chiseled and focused. He grabbed her wrist, drew her hand lower, and wedged it between them. "Play with yourself."

"I can't." Her body wrenched away without her permission.

"Do it."

She liked the command. The intensity in his eyes as he watched her. Despite her tender clit, she pushed past the brink of discomfort, and crested a new high, with him rocking inside her. It summoned another orgasm faster than she expected, and she dug her free hand into his bicep, needing something to ground her in the *now* before her head floated away.

He pounded, fast and steady, grunts punctuating each thrust. She recognized the sound from the other night. The tantalizing groans that teased her at the end of sleep. The sound that meant he was close. When he jackhammered frantically, then eased off with a long sigh, she swore she felt him spill inside her, though she knew that wasn't possible.

He hovered above her, as they struggled to catch their breath. She propped herself up on her elbows. Her legs weren't taking her anywhere for a while, so it was a good thing she didn't have to stand. She kissed and licked a trail up his chest, slid along his collarbone, memorizing the faint tang of salt and skin, and then pressed her lips to his.

When he slid out of her, he rolled to the side and took her with him. She lay there, curled up against him, listening to his heart, until the chill won out over the heat of sex, and she shivered.

"Stay right here." He gave her another kiss, stood, and wobbled, before he caught his balance.

At least she wasn't the only one their sex had that impact on. Orange flickered across his bare back and ass, and then on his semi-erect cock, when he returned seconds later with a heavier blanket, some pillows, and a large bottle of water.

He handed her the water, a glint in his eye. "The fire won't keep us warm all night. We're going to need a Round Two."

She laughed and sidled next to him under the blanket. "I definitely like the way you think."

* * * *

Mercy relaxed into the string of kisses Ian laid along the back of her neck. "New favorite way to wake up," she said. She could have sworn she felt him smile against her shoulder.

"Better than the cackle of chickens in Uruguay?"

Since last night, the fire had faded to embers. The storm howled against the sides of the house, blowing fresh snow into the windows and piling it up, but at least the power was back. Mercy wasn't in any hurry to get up. It was warm in Ian's arms. Comfortable and familiar, though they'd never done this. "Don't know. I never went to Uruguay. Do they have chickens there?"

"I think they have chickens everywhere." His warm breath fell against her bare back with each word, and he drew loops along her hip with his thumb. "Except maybe Antarctica."

She ground her ass back into him, a new kind of heat filling her when he hardened instantly. "Is this where one of us makes a bad pun about cocks?"

"I think the innuendo is better than the reality here. Let's pretend one of us did, and move on." He glided his hand forward, along her pelvis, and she arched her back into him. He teased along the top of her thigh, his touch somewhere between tickling and moan-inducing.

The shrill sound of a cell phone punctuated the air—digital and bell-like. Not hers. "Do you need to get that?" She hated to ask; she wanted to sink into this moment a bit longer.

"They'll wait." He slid his palm up her stomach, to her breast, and dragged a finger over one nipple. With each new touch, dampness grew between her legs.

The ringing died after a few seconds, and Ian increased the pressure of his playing.

Another ring greeted them, this time sounding like a land-line. She closed her eyes and nudged him back with her shoulder. "It's probably important, Mr. high-demand."

His growl rumbled through her back, and he kissed her shoulder one more time before pulling away. "I'm sorry."

"Go. See who it is." She rolled onto her back when Ian pulled away, and turned to watch him. He paused by the couch long enough to pull on his jeans. Watching him dress wasn't as much fun as undressing him, but it was still pretty good.

He glanced over his shoulder. "Enjoying the show?"

"I am." She snaked her arm down her stomach, still hidden by the blanket. "Too bad you have to take that call, or I'd give you one too."

"You're going to be my undoing. Don't touch yourself while I'm gone."

"Or what?"

"Or I won't have anything to do when I get back."

She laughed and nodded toward the doorway. "An effective threat. Don't make me wait?"

"Only long enough that you squirm and beg." His cell phone rang again, and he grabbed it from the end table. "This is Ian Thompson." His voice faded as he strode out of the room.

She studied the ceiling, letting lazy thoughts and pleasant images from last night keep her company. Minutes ticked away, and the past butted in as a chill crept over her. The times she and Liz had slept in this living room. The nights she'd lain awake, studying the exposed wood beams, wishing she didn't have to go home in the morning, and wondering if each footstep above them was Ian.

She'd been so head-over-heels back then. Another reason she was grateful he told her *no* when she asked to leave with him. She'd gotten him out of her system. Learned how much happier she was, standing on her own. When this week was over—hell, when the day was over—she'd go back to her life, and he'd go back to his, and that would be that. The pit in her chest told her that wasn't true; she'd still miss him. She argued it was easy to say that when they hadn't finished what they started this morning.

The clock on the wall said he'd been gone almost forty-five minutes. Long call. She shrugged off the blanket and went in search of her clothes. She found his sweatshirt first. The faint but heady scents of pine and musk settled over her, and she pulled it on. It barely covered her ass. Perfect.

She padded through the house, ears straining until she heard his voice drifting from the study. She approached the doorway and paused when his distinct words greeted her. "I understand your concerns, Mr. Woodhouse." His tone was cool. Professional and confident. "When you're in the offices tomorrow, you'll see we've addressed them." His back was to her.

Her stomach twisted in on itself. She didn't know how many Woodhouses there were out there, but it wasn't a name she'd come across very often. It was, however, the name of the marketing director for KaleidoMation—the account she hoped would take her company to the next level. Maybe it was coincidence. *Please let that be the case.*

"I assure you, we've got social media covered." Ian turned, smiling when he saw her. "We've got experts on staff, and we're talking to an independent contractor as well."

She didn't want to hear this. She'd walk away, wait in the living room until Ian was done, and then tell him they were each other's competition. He gestured for her to come closer, and she shook her head.

"The snow is perfect for it." Ian crossed the room in a few brief strides and grabbed Mercy's wrist before she could leave. "Fresh powder falling right now. If you're staying for the weekend, we'll hit the slopes together."

His grip was loose. She could wrench away. It might look a little melodramatic, but he'd understand once she explained her reasons.

"I'll have Jake keep an eye on the storm warnings, but I expect travel restrictions to be lifted by this afternoon. I'm sorry you were delayed a day, but we're ready for you whenever you arrive." Ian pulled her closer, wrapped an arm around her waist, and dragged his nose up the side of her neck.

God. That felt so good. She leaned into him and the gesture. He was almost done, anyway. It wouldn't hurt to hang out.

"Of course. We'll see you tomorrow. Have a safe flight."

Behind her, something made a *splunk* sound, like a phone hitting a leather seat. "You wear this better than I do." Ian brushed her hair aside and kissed along her shoulder. "Though the office is closed for the day, and everyone's working remotely, so you won't be wearing it for long."

She was about to spoil his mood. Probably forever. Not that it mattered; their fling already had an expiration date. It had moved up a few days, was all. She braced herself for what she had to say next, burned the sensation of his lips on her skin into her thoughts, and said, "We have to talk."

Chapter Twelve

We have to talk. Ian usually didn't mind that phrase. He'd delivered it himself, and he hadn't been attached enough to anyone who said it to him. This time, it clenched like a fist around his lungs. He hated to admit it, but this whole thing—a fling; a series of one-night stands; whatever they decided to call it— was starting to mean more to him. Maybe it was a good thing she was doing this now, so they could put distance between them before she went back home.

"Are we breaking up?" He kept his tone light, despite the sludge creeping inside. "Because I think we'd have to be dating first." *Fuck it.* The resolution bounced in his head. He wasn't letting her do this. There was a connection between them, and he didn't know how deep it ran, but he wasn't willing to cut things off before he found out.

"We *would* have to be." She stepped out of his grasp and turned to face him. "And no. This is business."

He didn't have a hard time reading her this morning, but wished he did. Her playful expression was gone, twisted and hidden under furrowed brows. She kept her gaze on his neck, rather than looking him in the eye. Something told him it wasn't the longer-than-expected phone call causing this. It might not even be her looming departure. "Tell me." He placed a finger under her chin and raised her head until he had her attention.

When she clenched her jaw and stepped out of reach, his muscles ratcheted a notch tighter.

She licked her lips, a motion that wasn't as seductive when she wore this scowl. "That big account I told you I was trying to land? The one that—" She clamped her teeth together and hissed. "Anyway—the work I'm doing while I'm up here? It's for KaleidoMation. Jonathan Woodhouse."

His brain stalled, but his mouth moved without his permission. "No worries, then. You can come consult for us." What the fuck was wrong with him?

"If you think you're being funny—which I hope is the case—you're not. If you're serious, I'll walk back to the hotel, to prove this conversation is over." She crossed her arms and took another step back.

At least he knew how to piss Mercy off in under two-point-five seconds. "Bad joke. Tasteless and not funny in any universe."

"But it meant you were thinking it."

"Of course I was. You heard me mention it to Woodhouse. I was going to ask you before I had any inkling this was the account you wanted."

Her shoulders relaxed, but the rest of her posture stayed the same. "It doesn't matter. I thought you should know, and I probably should find a ride back to the hotel anyway. I'll call their shuttle. The storm is easing up."

"Stop." He closed the distance between them, pulled her arms apart, and tangled his fingers in hers. "This doesn't have to change anything."

"Landing this account is huge for me. Career making. I told you that. You being my competition changes *everything*." Still, she didn't pull out of his grasp.

"Do you want me to walk away? Because it's big for me too."

She twisted her face into a mask of disbelief. "No. I'm not saying that. Not even implying it. Even if I thought you'd forgive me for making such a request, that's not how I land clients. It doesn't matter. We weren't going to last past this week, anyway."

"You really feel that way?"

"It's what we promised." She squeezed his fingers tighter.

He risked pulling her to him, and stopped with a few inches between them. "Things change. We've changed."

"Not when something like this pops up, they don't."

"If you hadn't overheard that call—better yet, if we weren't competing for the same contract—and I asked you to give *us* a chance, would you consider it?"

She scrubbed her face with her free hand. "That's not a fair question. It's not reality."

"Then answer hypothetically." Instinct and experience told him to stop pushing the issue. A louder voice insisted he'd never forgive himself if he walked away. "And honestly."

"I can't lie to you, Ian."

"All right. Let's change the hypothesis. We both move forward like we planned to. We don't talk business with each other—we weren't sharing details anyway. We don't pull our punches, but we don't fight dirty."

She raised her brows and pursed her lips. "And at the end of it all, there are no hard feelings or accusations?"

"Exactly." He could tell she didn't believe it was possible, and he didn't blame her. There had to be a balance, though. "We celebrate the winner's success and commiserate with second place."

"And you even managed to avoid saying *loser*." Some of the lines around her eyes faded, but didn't vanish. "You really know this sell-to-people-using-psychology shit."

The implication dug deep. "I'm not trying to manipulate you. And you still haven't given me an answer, but"—he squeezed her hand and held up their intertwined fingers—"this makes me think you haven't written the idea off yet."

"Why are you trying so hard?" She looked frustrated but didn't sound upset.

"Why aren't you?"

"It's been two nights. That doesn't mean anything. Two months don't mean anything. You can't form a bond like that."

"Maybe. Maybe not. But every relationship has to start somewhere. Either they end or keep going, but there's no point in stopping one simply because it didn't pop into existence six months into the experience."

"That barely makes any sense."

"Yes or no?"

"Yes." She met his gaze. "We'll keep business and pleasure separate, and I won't write us off yet. But in a week, I'm still going back home. I'm not a hopeless romantic, and I'm not giving up my business for something sappy like romance. You won't either, when it comes down to it."

He wrapped an arm around her waist and kissed her forehead, then her cheek, and down to her mouth. She relaxed against him with a tiny sigh. Was she right? What would he choose if it came down to her or the family business? Not that the company was on the line. "I'll drive you back to the hotel, so I know you're safe. We'll get our work done in separate buildings, and we'll have dinner tonight."

She rested her cheek against his chest. "You've got this all planned out, huh?"

"I'm playing it by ear." And hoping it didn't bite one or both of them in the ass. Or heart. He just had to be sympathetic when she lost the contract. No gloating. No pity offers of collaboration. Just sympathy.

She was good. His people were better.

* * * *

The honeymoon suite was astoundingly quiet when no one was around. Mercy settled into one of the overstuffed couches, adjusted her laptop on her legs, and poised her fingers over the keyboard. Like every time she'd repeated the gesture over the last couple of hours, she only got a few words in, before her thoughts drifted back to Ian. She was worse than fifteen-year-old her. Swooning over a guy. Letting him run rampant through her thoughts.

Agreeing to maybe-kind-of date, despite the fact they wouldn't last and regardless of how she knew he'd react when he lost the contract.

It didn't matter if he was Ian or the Dalai Lama; no one took that kind of defeat with grace. The stuff his firm turned out was decent, but she and her crew were flexible rather than unyielding, and that contract would be hers.

The latch on the door rattled, and Mercy muttered under her breath, "Do not disturb means do not disturb." She pasted on a smile for housekeeping and wondered why they hadn't knocked first.

Before she could ask, the door swung open, and Liz stepped into the room, shopping bags in hand. "Honey, I'm home." Her grin was wide and as vibrant as the sun striking the fresh snow outside. She stepped aside and nodded to an empty spot on the floor. "You can put those there." A porter moved around her, settled several shopping bags, and straightened. Liz slipped him a tip, then turned back to Mercy when he was gone. "Miss me?"

"Of course." Mercy hoped her smile looked genuine. She was happy to see Liz and had been worried about her. Guilt seeped in that she was a little disappointed Liz hadn't stayed in Salt Lake one more night. "Good trip?"

Liz's sunshine face drooped for a second, before returning full force. "Fantastic. I got so much new stuff, and… You know what? You're working. It'll wait."

"Okay." Mercy didn't want to argue. It was a fantastic offer. But the sharp contrast to the Liz who pouted because Mercy wouldn't go shopping with her was disconcerting. "I can take a break for a couple of minutes. I *am* here with you." She hadn't been getting much done anyway, but Liz didn't need those details.

"Did you get a lot done yesterday?" Liz sat next to her on the couch but didn't lean back and relax.

"Until the power went out."

"That sucks. The hotel has backups, right? I can't imagine they don't."

There was no reason for Mercy to stall. Even without the full story, her sleepover last night made sense. "I was at Ian's still, and the roads got bad up here."

"Oh, yeah. I get that." Liz's spine straightened further. If that was even possible. "Blankets and pillows by the fireplace, like when we were kids?"

Mercy tried to give her a reassuring grin, but whatever had Liz on edge mingled with Mercy's looming anxiety and marched like ants under her skin. She wasn't sure how much or what else to say. *We're dating now. FYI.* That wasn't true. *We're fucking, with potential for more.* Because hints of that went over so well last time. "Pretty much."

"Sounds like fun. I'm sorry I missed it. Really, you should get back to work."

Mercy gave her another curious glance. "If you're sure…"

"Of course." Liz hopped to her feet and grabbed a few bags. "I'll go in the bedroom. Watch a movie. I think I've had enough snow for now."

Mercy's tension wasn't passing anytime soon. She set her laptop on the coffee table and closed the lid. "What's up?"

"Nothing. A long couple of days. I need some rest."

"No, really. Tell me."

Liz flopped into an easy chair and dropped her face into her hands, muffling a sigh. "Do you like your job?" Her words ran together and sifted through her fingers.

Odd direction to take things. "Like, as a general rule? Since I made it for myself, I'm pretty fond of it, even when it's stressful."

"Was it hard to learn?" Liz's question was quiet, and though she removed her hands, she kept her gaze focused on the carpet. "I mean, not that I think what you do would be easy or anything. I know it takes a lot of work, but… is it something someone else could learn?"

Mercy struggled to figure out the direction of the questions. She watched Liz study the room around them, as if the white furniture and soft frills held answers. "Probably. People do it all the time. Ian learned. The people who work for me did."

"Do you think I could do it?" Liz looked up.

Mercy almost had an idea of where this was going now, but not why. "Be more specific? There are a lot of different things we do, but I'm sure you'd do great at whatever you picked."

"He had two fiancées in other parts of the country."

And the subject had changed again. Mercy tried to switch gears. "Ian?"

"Wouldn't surprise me. But I mean George. That's what the lawyer told me on Tuesday, he'd uncovered it in his research. George preys on socialites with inheritances. Women who don't have careers. I wasn't even *the other woman*. I fit a fucking profile. A stereotype. Even Ian knew it. He told me to make sure George was on the up-and-up, but I thought my heart knew better. No, I'm just a poor little rich girl who wanted to get married and have her man take care of her."

Mercy couldn't ignore Liz's bitterness. "That's not you."

"It *is* me. The only job I've ever had was sorting papers for Dad. And that was so I could say on my college application that I'd worked."

"But you're more than that."

"Am I?" Liz's question hung heavy with despair.

"Of course you are." Mercy didn't have to search for a response; she knew it was true. "You went to school. You got your MBA. You graduated at the top of your class. That was all you."

"To take my mind off losing my first husband. Once college was over, the moment another guy came along who smiled at me and knew the right words, I fell into a relationship again. I don't know how to be me."

Mercy's heart snagged at the despair in Liz's voice. "What do you want to be doing?" Mercy poured sympathy into her question. She knew what it was like to be lost. Just because she'd done it half a lifetime ago didn't meant she'd forgotten.

"You could hire me."

Mercy's answer stuck in her throat. That came out of left field. "Doing what?"

"I don't know. Getting coffee. Learning the ropes. My degree is in finance. I could do your books."

That was tempting. Mercy hated doing books and couldn't afford an accountant. But— "I don't have an office or the budget for a new employee. I'm sorry, hon." When Liz's bottom lip stuck out, Mercy added, "I'm not brushing you off, but I'm barely making it."

"No, that's okay. I'll be an intern. They don't get paid, right? And if I help you start making more money, you can put me on the payroll?"

"Interns are fresh out of college. I can't *not* pay you." Mercy hated telling her *no*. Liz would help her out if she needed it. She insisted on wiring Mercy money a couple of times, even when Mercy said she'd find a way. Gave her a safe-haven, growing up. "Ask Ian for a job," Mercy said.

A scowl spread over Liz's face. "You wouldn't."

"I don't need to."

"We both know what happens if I go to him. He won't hesitate. He'll give me a big title and fancy office, and piddly bullshit work."

It sounded so condescending when she put it that way. Mercy wanted to argue that wasn't the Ian she knew, but it clicked in her head and gnawed at her stomach. This *was* him, when it came to Liz. "I don't have a lot of time to train you. You'll have to do a lot of studying by yourself, to get up to speed."

"I will. I promise. I'll devour whatever you tell me to."

Mercy didn't think she'd regret the extra help. Liz was capable of doing what Mercy was about to ask, but Mercy did feel guilty about the lack of salary. And the nagging, telling her this might be a bad idea for reasons she hadn't considered. That was okay; she'd deal with it when the time came.

"We'll make it official, then. You get the same contract as everyone else. Follow the same rules, no favoritism."

"I promise." Liz grinned. "Thank you. Thank you, thank you. Now, finish your work, so we can go celebrate."

"Eh…" *Fuck*.

"Hmm?" Liz raised her brows.

"Ian and I are going to dinner. We thought you'd be in Salt Lake one more night."

Liz's smile fell from her eyes, but not her face. "No worries. He can celebrate with us. But you have to let me tell him."

Mercy gave a non-committal shake-nod. "Let me wrap up. He'll be here at seven." And then everyone could figure out what to tell everyone else. It'd be fun.

Chapter Thirteen

Ian knocked on the door of the honeymoon suite, and his pulse thrummed in his ears. When did he last anticipate a date this much? He couldn't say. With Liz gone for the night, Mercy had the place to herself. Maybe it was a good time to try out the amenities. Sure, he had a hot tub back at the house, but this one was en-suite, and hotel sex felt naughtier by default.

His evening planning stalled until it evaporated when the door swung open and Liz stood on the other side, dressed for what he assumed was dinner. "Hey." She beamed and pulled him into the room. "One more minute, and we'll be ready."

For the second time in just a couple of days, disappointment welled inside at seeing her and was quickly joined by guilt. Wait. *We'll* be ready? He was grateful she was back safe. That didn't mean he was changing his plans for her.

Mercy stepped into the room behind Liz, and mentally, Ian's jaw dropped. The high collar on her dress highlighted her neck, and the sleek curves hugged hers, the dress ending halfway down her thighs. In those heels, she had to be as tall as him. She smiled at him over Liz's shoulder. "Ready. And guess who's coming with us."

"Fantastic." Ian kept his irritation in check, not understanding where the sudden surge came from. His fingers twitched by his side, as nervous energy danced through them. He held open the door and bowed at the waist, gesturing to the hallway. "After you, ladies."

When they reached the parking lot, Liz jumped into the front seat the moment Ian held the door open. When Mercy slid into the back, he couldn't resist drawing in a lungful of her intoxicating scent. He dipped his head close to her ear, and whispered, "You could have warned me."

She gave him an apologetic shrug. "She wanted to surprise you."

He felt like he was being set up. The chatter on the way to the restaurant was light and simple. What Liz bought on her shopping trip. What the weather would be like for Mercy's trip. Ian wanted his conversations with Mercy back—sharing moments from their past, swapping jokes. Diving past the superficial.

"Are you all right?" Liz asked at one point.

He glanced in her direction while they waited for the light to change. "Fine. Why?"

"Your knuckles are white from gripping the steering wheel too hard."

That explained why his fingers ached. "Still tense about driving conditions."

Things didn't improve much once they reached their destination and were seated. The biggest difference was, now that the two women faced each other, he could see the shared looks, the clamped lips, and the occasional, almost imperceptible shake of

Liz's head, in response to a question in Mercy's gaze. Even if he hadn't spent half his teenage years watching them do this, he'd know they were hiding something.

Was it about Mercy and him? They should have discussed whether or not they were telling Liz. Whatever this was, though, it was Liz's secret though. "What else is new?" he asked her.

"I was only gone a day or so." Liz spoke from behind her drink, the wine glass muffling her words, and she wouldn't make eye contact. "I'm still single and heartbroken. But tomorrow I'm looking at condos, so at least I won't be homeless."

"You're looking at condos. In a ski-resort town in February." He let disbelief slide into his words.

She fiddled with her ring finger, which was sans engagement ring. "I'm not an idiot. They'd bleed me dry on rent. I'm looking at places in Salt Lake, maybe even Ogden. I've got work prospects."

Mercy tightened her jaw, and Ian raised his brows. *Interesting.* "What's going on?" He made sure not to direct the question at anyone specifically.

Mercy glanced at Liz, who finally looked at him. "Nothing. Coping with reality. I have to do it sometime, you know?"

"I have to make a business call." Mercy stood so abruptly, her chair legs scraped across the tile. "I'm sorry to interrupt, but it's urgent and I forgot."

The bread had just arrived. Fuck, Ian couldn't do this all night. "What are you two hiding?" he asked Liz, instead of giving into the impulse to watch Mercy's ass as she strode away.

"Nothing." Liz was back to studying her butter knife. "Don't know what you're talking about."

In the background, the soft clatter of silverware against china filtered in to fill the silence. "Liz."

"What? It's— I mean— Nothing."

She was mourning. She was left at the altar less than a week ago. A woman had a right to her secrets. That didn't stop Ian from being grateful when his phone buzzed. "It's Jake. I'll be back in a few. Start without me if Mercy and the appetizers get back before I do." He was scanning through the messages as he strode away, not waiting for Liz's response.

Jake's text was standard information. *Woodhouse's flight is in. I've dropped him off at the hotel. We're set for tomorrow.*

Ian didn't have to walk away to talk, but it was as rude to text at the table as it was to take a call. Besides, he needed some air. Something was fucking with his head, testing his patience when he didn't have a right to be irritated, and he needed to eliminate it. He sent Jake back a quick, *Thanks. See you in the morning,* and set his phone to Do Not Disturb, so only calls and messages flagged as *priority* would come through.

The restaurant had their wine racks and a pastry counter in a room separate from everything else, on the other side of the lobby. He didn't want to leave Liz alone for long, but he saw the perfect solution to unfogging his thoughts. At the far end, out of sight of everything but the entrance, Mercy stood next to the window, staring into the night.

He strode up behind her and wrapped an arm around her waist. She started, and then leaned into him. "I was about to head back." Her quiet words mingled with the music drifting from hidden speakers.

"You two are hiding something." That wasn't what he meant to say. A trend he noticed more and more when she was around.

She turned to face him, and he encircled her hips, resting his hands against her back. She draped her arms around his neck. "You and I are hiding something from her, too. That makes everything even."

"No. That means you know all the secrets." He nipped at her bottom lip. "Speaking of, why are *we* a secret?"

She pressed closer and glided her nails along the back of his neck. "What do you propose we say? She already thinks we'd be bad for each other. *Jaded* meets *cynical*, and all that. I'm not sure, *Hey, we're screwing and maybe more but maybe not*, is going to change her mind." She kissed him, mouth soft and yielding, the faint tart of wine still on her lips. He spun her and guided her to the wall, so he could lean into her.

It was so easy to lose himself in this. She shifted her weight, rubbing against his cock, and he glided his hand lower, over her ass and past the hem of her skirt.

She laughed against his mouth. "Not in here."

"Car's outside."

"Liz is waiting for us." She tilted her head and sighed when he kissed down her throat.

He skimmed over her collar and met skin again when he reached her shoulder. "Speaking of. What's she keeping from me?"

"You'll have to ask her."

He teased along the inside of Mercy's thighs with one hand and twisted the fingers of the other in her hair. He crushed his mouth to hers, hungry, wanting to dive into her. He was rock hard and digging into her stomach.

His phone vibrated in his jacket pocket. She nudged him away, disappointment in her tiny laugh. "I should get back to the table." When she brushed past him, she traced his shaft through his slacks. "See you in a few minutes."

He whirled and rested against the wall. *Hey, we're screwing and maybe more but maybe not.* It echoed in his thoughts. Why hadn't he thought things through better, before doing any of this with Mercy? She had a way of making him forget consequences mattered. Instead of bothering him, the notion made his pulse race and his adrenaline climb. She had a good point about telling Liz, though. He'd told himself that first night he wouldn't be a rift in their friendship. Wouldn't hurt his sister. And he would stand by that decision.

He forced thoughts of bitter cold, tax season, and FCC audits through his head, until his erection ebbed enough that he could walk without adjusting himself every step, then checked his phone to see what kind of emergency waited for him. It was a message from Liz. *You all right?*

That was one way to kill a hard-on. He didn't reply. Both women were back at the table when he returned. He needed to be a better sport about the evening. He and Liz had always been close, and he didn't want to jeopardize that.

"How's work?" Liz asked.

"Same as always. Speaking of—you said you had prospects? I didn't know you were looking."

Mercy sighed. "Just tell him. It's not a celebration if one member of the party doesn't know."

Liz twisted her napkin in her lap. "I'm not looking. I found something."

"That's fantastic. Doing what?" Fleeting concern ached behind his ribs.

"Whatever Mercy needs me to."

That explained the shared looks. "You could have come to me. You know—*Thompson Advertising*? *Your* name's on the logo, too. We have an office we can put you in—"

"I have a job." Liz clipped off each word. "Starting in accounting and moving up from there."

How had he gotten backed into a corner so quickly? And why did he care who she worked for? Because Mercy was the competition. Except she wasn't, and the furrow of her brows said she didn't like the turn the conversation took. He glued on a smile. "That came out wrong. I meant to say *congratulations*. I think it's a fantastic reason to celebrate."

"Really?" Liz hopped from her chair, leaned over, and gave him a huge hug. "Thank you. I'm really excited about it."

Mercy's smile didn't come so easily. She fiddled with a piece of bread, not looking at either one of them.

Finding out if he and Mercy could have more was going to be a lot more complicated than he thought, and it had been less than a day.

Chapter Fourteen

Liz had her door open almost before Ian's SUV stopped rolling, when he pulled up in front of the hotel. Mercy felt like a teenager, and not in a good way, at the quick hug Liz and Ian exchanged. This was a bond Mercy would never come between.

When she slipped into the conversation Liz didn't approve of anything happening between Mercy and Ian, she tried to fight her disappointment, and failed. Mercy wanted him to say it didn't matter what Liz thought. She knew better, though. Childish expectations, all over again.

She hopped from the car.

"Mercy." Ian's voice made her pulse skip and her heart patter. Damn him. "Can I borrow you for a moment?" He stood next to the driver's side of the vehicle. "I have a business question."

Mercy glanced at Liz, who waited near the hotel entrance. "Five minutes," Mercy said. "I'll be right up." She waited until Liz was inside and out of sight, before joining Ian.

Ian grabbed Mercy's hand and pulled her close, mostly hidden from view of the building, and her heartbeat cranked another notch.

"This is a bad idea." He settled his hands at her hips.

"Making out in the freezing cold?"

"Hiring Liz."

Her building blood pressure ratcheted for a new reason. "*We*—you and I—don't talk business. Also, this isn't your call."

"I don't mean—" He clenched his teeth and sucked in the air through them. "If you want to keep us a secret, that makes it harder to do. I'm not trying to butt into your business or her life. My hesitation revolves around you and me."

Mercy had her doubts, but there was no animosity in his words. "What are we going to tell her? That we're fuck buddies for the next two or three days?"

"Do you really think that?"

She had to. What other option was there? Anything else was unrealistic. An immature fantasy she wouldn't let distract her if he was anyone else. "I can't think of it as more."

"Why not?"

"Don't make me answer that." How was she supposed to explain?

He brushed his lips over hers. A feather-light graze that sent pleasant chills over her skin. "I'm not asking you to define anything," he said. "Just to not write us off yet."

"I leave for my meeting with KaleidoMation Monday morning." She stepped back but still held his hand.

He gave her fingers a final squeeze before letting go. "I know. The clock's ticking in my head, even without the reminder. Good night, Mercy."

Confusion mingled with irrationality, while she rode the elevator up. When she left home, the theory was there in her head—sex and love could be separate. Not interested in the local guys, she'd never put it into practice, but she knew she could do it. Until she hooked up for the first time. Lost her virginity to a stranger in a bar in Venezuela. She knew she was in love. It didn't help that he muttered things like, *I love you, baby*, every time they fucked, for almost a week straight.

When he left, reminding her it was just a fling, she curled in on herself for about half a day, until she remembered that wasn't her. Now she was inches from making a similar mistake with Ian, because of who he was—tied to a memory and a portion of her past she thought she'd shed years ago.

She reached the room and was surprised to see most of the lights out. The door to the bedroom was closed, no glow spilling from underneath. She knocked.

"Sleepy. Tomorrow?" Liz called back.

"Yeah." Mercy settled on the couch, not bothering with lamps or changing out of her dress. She tugged her knees to her chest and tried to make sense of the jumble inside. It didn't matter how many arguments part of her presented, she always ended up at the same end point. Ian was temporary. There were too many reasons for him to never be more.

Which didn't stop her from hating the way she left things with him. She pulled her phone from her purse, and sent him a text. *Good luck with Jonathan tomorrow.*

Might as well get some sleep. His answer buzzed through seconds later. *Is that all I get?*

She smiled, in spite of herself. The only other thing she could think of was, *I miss you.* Going down that road was dangerous. Instead she settled for, *Did you have something else in mind?*

I believe there was mention of pictures.

She never should have told him those existed. There were no photos. She hated having her picture taken. *Your mention, not mine.*

That's fair. And it's my mention again, he replied. *But I won't see you until Sunday. Send me something to keep me company.*

Her chaotic thoughts twisted another degree toward out of control. His request thrummed through her veins, pulsing with excitement and the wickedness of it all. How did he do this to her? One minute she doubted every aspect of their relationship. The next, with a single request, he made her wonder how much she was comfortable showing him. Hesitation and self-doubt won out. Her text said, *Not tonight.*

I understand. You'll be in my dreams anyway.

She stared at the message far longer than she should. What was she doing?

* * * *

"How do you do it?" Liz picked at the leftover blueberries from her now-gone muffin. They sat at a table outside the hotel coffee shop, watching the afternoon tourists walk by.

Mercy paused her drink, straw halfway to her mouth. "Manage payroll for all of seven people? I think you've got the basics down." They were discussing an accounting timeline and what Liz needed in order to slide into the position. The conversation included Liz looking at the budget and making suggestions on ways to get her salary paid. She might be okay with working for free, but Mercy wasn't going to allow it.

"Spend time with a guy—any guy—sleep with him, talk to him, enjoy his company, and then walk away when it's all done, like nothing happened."

"Sometimes it's harder than others. Depends on the guy." Mercy whispered a short prayer that this wasn't heading toward a very specific conclusion.

"How difficult will it be with Ian?" Liz looked up, eyes wide and innocent, the rest of her expression blank.

And there it was. *More difficult than it should be.* "I don't know. How long have you…?"

"I had a feeling after the whole I-spent-the-night-and-we-have-dinner-plans thing. Your lipstick was smudged last night when you came back to the table. And on his collar."

That actually happened? Mercy didn't notice before. She also had no idea what to say.

"Do me a favor?" Liz said.

"Always."

"Please don't let him break you this time." Liz crumpled her empty wrapper and napkin into a tiny ball and stood.

What the hell? Irritation and curiosity spilled through Mercy. She grabbed Liz's wrist and rose, as her friend walked by. "You don't walk away after a statement like that. I've got this."

Liz's shoulders rose and fell, and she turned back to Mercy. "I was there the first time. I watched you swoon over him and worship him, and withdraw when he left. For a long time, I thought I lost you. After you left, you started to come back around. I watched you change through the emails and the phone calls, and who you were shone through again."

"Are you sure that's what your problem is?" Mercy should have let it go, but every time Liz had slipped in something passive aggressive over the past few days flitted back to taunt her. "Not that I'm not good enough for your brother?" Forcing the question out scraped her throat raw. She didn't want to believe it or even think it, but now she'd said it, she realized it had lingered in the back of her mind since the morning after the failed wedding.

Was that really only five or six days ago?

"No. *Heavens* no." Liz twisted her hand until she was holding Mercy's instead of being her captive. "I meant what I said at the bar. I don't know how you let the world rush around and over you, while you stand unflinching in the middle. I worship you. I adore you."

Mercy struggled to process the confession. "I don't—"

"I'm not done. You built your business from the ground up. You're strong. You're independent, and before Ian dug into your head as a teenager, you took the world at face value. Ian will destroy that. Again." There was no venom in her words. Only sadness and surrender.

"God, Liz. He's your brother."

"He is. And I love him dearly. I trust him with my life and with everything else in the world. Except you. Because I love you more." Liz rose on her toes and kissed Mercy on the lips. Tentatively and softly, but then with more power.

Shock pushed everything else out of Mercy's head. The kiss was good. On a physical level, it sang to her senses and shoved the rest of the world aside. The spark wasn't there, though. And holy fuck, what had Liz just said? Mercy assembled enough sense to break the contact and gently push Liz back. "Where did this come from?"

"You've been with women before."

Mercy shook her head spinning her thoughts up. Making sense of the situation. Realizing she'd have to tell Liz she wasn't interested. How had she not seen this coming? "That's not what I asked."

"I've thought about it before; it's not new." Liz furrowed her brow and twisted a strand of hair around her finger—a nervous habit she'd had forever. "But I never wanted to accept I might like more than just men. This crap with George, though, and having you here... We've been there for each other since we met. You love me too. You've said so."

"I do, but not like that, hon."

"So you love Ian instead?"

"I don't know. No. Probably not." Mercy struggled to find the words to make things right. "What happened with George has to be hard. You haven't mourned yet. I know you've let yourself cry a couple of times, but not really."

"*Damn it.*" Liz's tone drew glances from nearby patrons. Pink flooded her cheeks. "Don't talk down to me like I don't get it." Her voice was softer again.

"I'm not. I'm just…" Mercy was going to have to be blunt and keep pushing until Liz got it. *Please let us recover.* "I don't feel that way about you. I'm sorry. You're still my best friend, and you mean the world to me. There's nothing romantic there, though."

"Then, the kiss?"

Mercy shook her head. "You're a good kisser."

"Fuck." Liz stared at her feet. "I guess that's something. Are you going to fire me now?"

"No. You're welcome to resign, but I hope you don't. What we accomplished today? More than I've gotten done in a month. And I mean that. I also won't pretend this didn't happen."

Liz stepped back, still studying the ground. "I think I need to go."

It wasn't a resolution, but Mercy didn't know what else to say.

"Is this the part where I run up to the room and you go spend the night with Ian?" Liz's question was so soft, Mercy had to strain to hear.

"I don't know. I hadn't thought past hoping this doesn't cost me your friendship."

Liz glanced up. "I need some time. I'll email you if I have work questions."

"Yeah. Okay." Mercy sank into her chair as Liz strode away at high speed. What now?

Chapter Fifteen

Ian shook Jonathan's hand. "I'll pick you up at seven."

"Sounds great." Woodhouse joined Jake at the front entrance to the office. It wasn't company policy to drive the client around, but with the weather as spotty as it was, Ian was happy to provide a temporary shuttle service. Especially if it looked better for Thompson Advertising when it came down to decision time.

The presentation had gone fantastically. Ian's Sales team pulled out all the stops, and from where he sat, addressed all the concerns they needed to. Something crawled under Ian's skin. Dissatisfaction? Concern? He was prepared to be sympathetic when Mercy lost the contract, but this was something else. He shook the feeling aside.

It was four now. Plenty of time to catch up on messages. A text from Liz waited for him, but she hadn't sent it *priority*—something she wouldn't hesitate to do. He'd get back to her after he sifted through voicemail and emails.

He put his phone on speaker and let the messages fill the room while he clicked through computer work. He made the occasional note, but most of it was informational.

"Ian, this is Dean Rice. Give me a call as soon as you have a moment. I'll be in the office late tonight."

Mercy's father. But also a client. Ian's fingers paused over the keyboard, and that same feeling from earlier surged back stronger but still as difficult to name. It was true, he attended lunches with local clients, but their account managers should be fielding their concerns. What had gone so wrong in the past few days that required him to be involved directly? He had Dean's number up and was dialing, even as the question circled in his thoughts.

"Ian. Good to hear from you. Thank you for calling me back." Dean's voice was warm, with no underlying hints of negativity.

"Of course. What can I do for you?"

Nervousness filled Dean's laugh. "You get straight to the point, don't you? Something I admire about you."

"I hate to keep you on longer than you have to be." Ian clenched and unclenched his fingers, trying to cast out the nervous energy coursing through him.

"I appreciate that. I, uh…" His hesitation set Ian further on edge. "I need a favor. I'd like to see Melissa again."

Ian muted the phone just in time to let out a long exhale of surprise. *Didn't see that coming.* And given the way Mercy reacted to her father the other day and the sideways mentions since, he suspected she didn't have the same desire to see Dean. "I'd still rather keep professional and personal separate. It's not my place to get involved in something like this. I hope you understand." An impulse filled him, trying to push out something less politically correct and more like, *and why would she want to see you?* He buried the thought.

"I'm not asking you as a client; I'm a father, asking one of his daughter's friends."

Maybe you should have considered that— Ian cut himself off. A second nagging voice pointed out he would have hated himself if he hadn't said *goodbye* to his parents. Mercy's family was different, though. *Fuck.* "I'm sorry."

"I understand." Resignation replaced Dean's cheer. "If you would, please tell her I asked and give her my number. Leave the rest up to her, and I won't bring it up again."

Indecision warred inside, but Ian finally said, "All right. I'll do that."

"Thank you."

Not what Ian expected. He shook his head and ended the call. He would have preferred an angry client call. He wrapped up the rest of his work, the non-stop question of whether or not to tell Mercy bouncing in his head the entire time. The images of Mercy, and almost knocked his focus offline. The way her naked body looked in the firelight. The gorgeously wrenching cries she made when she came. And he wouldn't see her again until Sunday. Maybe she'd make time for him Saturday afternoon?

He gave his to-do list one last glance, making sure everything that couldn't wait until Monday was done, and pulled up Liz's message.

Heads-up—I've got a hotel in Salt Lake. I'm staying down here until I find a new place.

That was abrupt. He asked, *Why the sudden departure? Room is paid for through the weekend.*

I need a change of scenery. Sorry for wasting your gift. It was just a text, so he expected short sentences and terse words, but this felt like something more.

I'm not concerned about the gift. Just you. What's up?

I'm fine, she said.

Is Mercy going with you? He waited for several seconds after the message. No answer. The clock ticked up on five, then ten minutes. *Liz?*

No.

His concern grew at the terse response. *Liz?*

Go meet with your client. Talk later.

He dialed her number and went to voicemail after only one ring. Great. She was screening him. He called Mercy next.

"Hey." Her greeting was strained.

"Are you with Liz?"

"No."

At least they had that in common. "Are you all right?" he asked.

"I'm fine. Busy with work. You know."

He needed to leave soon, to pick up Woodhouse, but the gnawing in his joints insisted he dig deeper on this. "How's Liz?"

A pause filtered over the line, and if it weren't for the faint whisper of her breath against the receiver, he'd wonder if he lost the call. "She's fine too."

"But you're not with her."

"And I haven't spent every waking moment with her. If you want to know how Liz is, call Liz." Tone of voice was a lot easier to gauge over the phone than text, and there was little room for misinterpretation in Mercy's response. "She's just in the other room."

"That's not what she tells me."

Mercy's sigh rocked his eardrums. "If you already knew the answer, why did you ask? Is this a new kind of game?" she asked.

"I don't know. Is it?" He didn't want to piss her off, but the avoiding questions and giving odd answers from both of them was rubbing him raw. "She texted me to say she was moving to Salt Lake. Tonight. Without you. Now you tell me she's in the other room."

Mercy gave a strangled laugh. "Tonight? Thanks for the info. I have work."

"*Mercy.* Tell me what's going on."

More silence, stretching over the line and buzzing in his ears. She finally said, "We need to talk."

And his tension cranked a notch higher. He'd snap a tendon in his neck at this rate. "I don't like it when you say that."

"Me neither. Not over the phone. I can't. But… Are you free tonight?"

"I'm taking Woodhouse to dinner." He seriously considered canceling. The two conversations slid through his veins like razors.

"Don't cancel. Can I see you after? I don't care how late it is."

He wasn't sure he'd make it through dinner, without having his questions answered. This lack of control gnawed at him. It was the best option, though. "Give me a couple of hours. I'll text you when I'm on my way to you."

* * * *

When Ian finally pulled up in front of the hotel, it was almost ten-thirty. He didn't know who he was more concerned about, Mercy or Liz.

Mercy was outside, pacing off to the side of the main entrance. She hopped into the car the moment he pulled up next to her, but she didn't meet his gaze. Her knee bounced, and she twisted her fingers together in random patterns. "Can we go somewhere that's not your place?"

"Where?"

"I don't know. For a drive? Is that place still in Heber City?"

"Yeah." He twitched with the need for answers. "Are you okay?"

"I need to sort it out before I can talk. Drive, please?"

He put the car in park, shifted in his seat, and cupped her cheeks between his palms. Any other time, he'd lean in and kiss her, but the way she darted her gaze everywhere, that desire took a back seat. "Hey." He kept his tone quiet but firm. "Look at me."

She focused on him, drumming her fingers on her knee.

"Are you all right?" Something invisible gripped his heart and squeezed. He wanted to fix this. Needed to make it better.

"Physically, yes. Mentally? God. I feel fucked up. Not here?"

He dragged a thumb across her cheek and searched her eyes one more time for answers they didn't hold, before letting her go. "We'll drive. Okay?"

She nodded.

"When we get there, we'll sit in the back corner, in the same booth as always, and we'll talk. You can tell me whatever you're comfortable with."

The moment overlapped a handful from their past. Except back then, it was always the pressure of her family and church. Now, he couldn't even begin to guess.

"Okay." Her voice was weak, and too much like teenage-her. He wasn't telling her about the call from Dean.

He pulled onto the road. Out of the corner of his eye, he saw her turn most of her body toward the window. It was as if she'd built a wall between them.

Twenty minutes later, they turned into the parking lot of a local twenty-four-hour diner. This time of night on a Friday, with nothing else in town open, cars filled almost every available space.

He found a spot, and Mercy was out of the SUV before he could shut off the engine. A blast of cold spilled over him when he moved to join her. She was pacing again. Watching her feet. Lips moving, but no sound coming out.

He leaned against the car and waited, ignoring the chill seeping through his coat.

"I'd tell Liz about this, but I can't." Her steps punctuated her words. "And I shouldn't talk to you. *God.* You're the last person I should dump this on, because Liz, your sister— You know? But you're the guy I'm fucking, so you kind of need to know, and I'm trying to sort this out in my head, and I can't."

He grabbed her fingers, icicles wrapped in flesh, and tugged her to a stop. "You don't have to sort it out. Spill whatever pops into your head or whatever you need."

She shook free. She took fistfuls of his jacket, drew close, and settled her forehead against his chest. She wasn't crying, as far as he could tell. He settled his hands at the small of her back.

Her voice was muffled when she spoke. "This is so fucked up. Like the-three-of-us-on-Montel kind of fucked up."

It had to be, at least a little, for her to be referencing old daytime talk shows. "What is?"

She looked up, eyes dry and bloodshot. "Liz kissed me."

"As in an, *O.M.G. I'm so excited—big hugs* kind of kiss?" He knew what she meant, but his brain refused to let him process it.

"No. As in, *I love you, promise me you feel the same.*"

He rested more of his weight against the car. "Fuck me."

"Yeah. That might have been a catalyst." A smile threatened to twitch onto her lips.

If she was making jokes, this was helping. Not him. He needed to wrap his head around it, but he felt more relief than he expected, to see her relaxing. "Then what?" She was right; this was borderline talk-show dysfunctional.

"I told her I didn't feel the same. She said she needed time to think." Mercy stepped away from him. "She asked if it would send me running into your arms. I guess it did."

That soothed him further. "You didn't technically *run*."

She stuck out her tongue. "This really is a mess."

"Come on. We'll go inside and sit and figure it out." He led her toward the entrance. It seemed as though pulling her out of her own head made the difference between crawling anxiety and coping.

Their table was free. Among crowded booths, packed with teenagers, the one at the back remained empty. Mercy looked him over, amusement creeping into her gaze. "You're a little overdressed."

"Luckily for me, there's no dress code." The light teasing was nice, but it left room for his questions to flood in. If Liz was gay, that was fine, though he'd never seen any hints. He wasn't that unobservant. His concern was what this would do to Liz. What it was doing to Mercy. He didn't want to come between them, and he definitely didn't want them to push each other away. Theirs was the kind of bond that shouldn't be screwed with.

The hostess let them have their booth, and Mercy slid into the seat facing the door. "There's nothing to figure out," she said. "I know the solution; I just don't like it."

"Oh?"

"Give her time to think, hope she forgives me for not feeling the same, and pray to anyone who's listening that our friendship survives."

What about us? He felt bad for the selfish thought, as soon as it manifested. At least this time he'd kept it to himself. "I didn't realize Liz was gay."

"I don't think she is." Mercy fiddled with her straw, poking at ice cubes in the water the waitress brought her. "She probably falls somewhere in the middle. Or I assume so, after today."

"Or you just have that effect on people." He poured the teasing into his words.

She looked up at him, lips drawn into a thin line. "You think you're funny. Or reassuring." Her scowl slipped. "I guess you are."

"Not that it matters who she likes. If she's okay, I'll let her be. And the two of you will work this out. I'm worried about *you*. Your state of mind."

Her smile returned, reaching her eyes this time. "I'll be okay."

"What can I do?" Wrap her up. Hold her. Chase this away.

"Distract me."

He could do that. He reached across the table, grasped her fingers, and worked some warmth back into them. "You asked about me the other day, and I kept turning things back on you. What do you want to know?"

Chapter Sixteen

Mercy wondered if she was being melodramatic. Overreacting to what happened with Liz. She sat outside the coffee shop for hours after they parted ways, trying to make sense of what happened and the jumble in her head. She kept coming back to the same thing. She'd tried so hard to keep her heart safe, and Liz was supposed to be the one person who wouldn't destroy it.

Which led to guilt—she was the one who turned Liz away. Which led to rationalization—she couldn't pretend her love for Liz was romantic. Which led her back to that same conclusion—this sucked.

When Ian called, she tried to block him out; his concern wasn't for her. Except she didn't know if she had the strength, and it added another layer to the mess inside her skull.

Now he sat across from her and let her lead the conversation, his attention for her alone. It helped. She was finally thinking straight.

It also ached through every inch of her. She was tired of keeping him out. It took so much effort, and she didn't know if she wanted to push him away anymore. At the same time, he wasn't a replacement for Liz, and she couldn't use him as if he were. How had the lines gotten so fuzzy and fucked up in such a short span of time?

He was going to distract her, talking about anything else. This was fine. And no sex. It would drill deeper into her thoughts than she could handle right now, and that was the reason she'd stay on her side of the table, instead of sliding in next to him.

She knelt on her bench seat and loosened his tie. This was about distraction. "Every time I see you, you're all suited up." She undid the top button on his shirt. Her fingers remembered. Wanted her to do more. She jerked away as subtly as she could and dropped onto the seat again.

"I came from work. Some of us have to deal with offices and suits."

Faulty logic. She could handle this. "It's your company. You could change the dress code."

"That's not how it's done. We have clients in the office on a daily basis."

The waitress strode by with two plates of burgers and fries, and Mercy's stomach growled. It was creeping up on midnight, and that muffin in the hotel was the last thing she ate. A two-second glance at the menu told her it hadn't changed much over time. Perfect. "Your clients probably don't wear suits back home either. Except maybe those legacy clients you kind of want to ditch, but that's not how it's done."

"Exactly." He laughed.

"So?"

He held out his hands in question, palms up. "I don't know what you're getting at."

"You really have changed." Keep it about him. Nothing else. Nothing to remind her of Liz. She'd deal with that in a little bit, but this helped her think again. "What happened to that guy who taught me about bucking authority and standing on my own?"

"I grew up, and the sucky thing is adulthood doesn't work that way." His words faded as he spoke, and he frowned.

"Mine does."

"Really?" His tone was flat.

"It's true I make concessions. The world has other people in it, and compromise is part of the deal. But I keep my office the way I want, I dress the way I want for work, and I don't take on the clients I don't want. One of the compromises of that is I have to be creative, to make ends meet, but for me, the freedom is more important than the money."

"And for me, taking care of the people I love is more important than the freedom."

"This is about Liz?" As soon as the name slipped past Mercy's lips, her gut sank. Maybe they couldn't keep that topic off the table. Would it be a problem, if they found a way to make *them* work? Might as well finish her thought. "She doesn't work for you. She has her own inheritance. Fuck, unless she quits"—the word choked off in Mercy's throat, and she swallowed past the lump it left—"because I know she won't screw up—I don't hire fuck ups— she's got her own job, outside of your firm."

"It's a family business."

Mercy turned her hands over and slid her palms under his. The warmth seeped into her, soothing the tiny fissures running through her thoughts. She knew this conversation. They'd had it over a decade ago, but she'd been in his shoes and her faith was in church instead of industry. "Is she the only reason you're doing things the way you are?"

"Of course not."

She didn't want him on the defensive. "I'm not trying to convert you. Or maybe I am. I see it when you talk about Thompson Advertising. There's this shadow of… I don't know. Regret?"

"You sound like me back then."

So she wasn't the only one who noticed the similarities. "Where do you think I got it? I just wish I knew why you lost it."

"I did what I had to do."

"Maybe it's time to make that decision again."

"It's not that easy anymore."

The waitress paused, to ask if they were ready, and Mercy ordered the biggest burger on the menu, with a chocolate shake. Ian only wanted *a Coke.*

"You don't have to starve yourself, to impress me," Mercy said as soon as the waitress left.

He relaxed a little. "Clever. Maybe I'm saving room for dessert." The way he dragged his gaze over her made her pulse race and her heart hammer against her ribs. It wasn't fair he could do that with a look.

It didn't change the situation. She shook her head. "I'm sorry. Not until… I don't know. I'm not in a good head space tonight."

"It's okay." There was no hesitation in the assurance. "I might steal some of your fries, though."

"Can I ask something in return? It's not really an equivalent exchange for fries—"

"You can ask me anything. No trade necessary."

She didn't doubt it for a moment, but she still felt guilt for this specific thing. "I don't know if I can sleep in that hotel room tonight. You said she won't be there, and I guess it's childish of me, but…" Jesus, it was as if she and Liz had broken up. Except this had to be temporary. *Please let it be temporary.*

"Stay with me." Ian stopped her before she could ramble. "That's not an innuendo-filled suggestion. The place has a billion and one guest rooms. Or a couple, and I promise they're more comfortable then hotel rooms."

* * * *

Ian needed to get up soon. He was supposed to be at the ski resort in two hours. Mercy's warm body against him made a convincing case for blowing the whole thing off. She muttered something that sounded like *too early* and pressed her panty-clad ass back into him.

And now he was hard. Damn it, this woman fucked with his head. Despite both of them agreeing she'd be happier in a guest room, talking had led them to his bed, and they both wanted her to stay when it got too late to stay awake.

He brushed her hair off her cheek and resisted the urge to draw his lips along the edge of her ear. He only slept in boxers, and she'd stripped out of her jeans, curled up against him, and passed out. It was so tempting to see if she was in a better mood this morning. To invite her to join him in the shower.

"I have to get ready. Sleep a little longer." He kissed her on the cheek and summoned more willpower than he thought he had, to roll away from her. Waking up next to her was comfortable. How could something he'd only done twice be so familiar?

Conflict raged inside, as he turned the shower on, shed the rest of his clothes, and stepped under the near-scalding spray. She'd shown no indication of changing her mind about her schedule. Not that he blamed her. She didn't live here, and she wasn't going to give up a life she earned, because of a whim and a few days of hot sex.

He knew there was more between them. As many times as one of them tried to pretend otherwise, the connection tugged him toward her. Last night was only one indicator of that. Even when they weren't doing anything but talking, he wanted her there.

Though the sex was incredible too. Memories streamed through his head. Vivid images, carried on the sound of her sighs. Her body yielding to his touch. The way her lips felt, wrapped around his cock. His fading erection roared back to life. He wrapped a soaped fist around it. Apparently he hadn't rid himself of the fantasy from waking up next to her.

The alternative played out in his thoughts as he stroked. Mercy grinding into him, nothing but a few thin layers of clothing keeping them apart. Him, reaching around her. Gliding a hand under her shirt. Her groans when he pinched her nipples. Slipping his hand between her legs from behind and pushing aside her panties. How wet she'd be.

His balls tightened, as the images grew more vivid. In his mind, she reached back and guided him in, shifting her position enough he penetrated her. Fingering her clit. The way she'd squirm and gasp, milking his cock, drawing out his climax. Screaming when she came. Fuck, he loved that sound.

He pumped faster, biting the inside of his cheek, to keep his grunts from carrying too far. Pressure built inside, and his head swam. He pounded his hand, jerking and yanking, until orgasm spilled through him, coating his hand and hitting the tile.

He finished his shower quickly, rinsing away the physical traces of fantasy and wishing it had cleared his head. He dried off and wrapped a towel around his waist. When he stepped into the master bedroom, Mercy sat at the edge of the mattress, dressed and tapping on her phone.

She looked up, a smile curling the corners of her mouth. "I was tempted to join you. I'm not sure if you know this, but that bathroom has some powerful acoustics."

Had she—?

"But it sounded like you took care of everything yourself." She had.

He appreciated how direct she was and how she expected the same from him. "I would have rather had the company." His cell-phone rang, shattering the playful mood.

She nodded toward where it sat on his nightstand. "Second time it's gone off. I'll give you some privacy." And with that, she strolled out of the room.

A glance at the phone told him it was Liz, and a new flavor of contention filled him. "Hey. I was worried about you."

"I figured." Liz's voice was tired and raspy. "Is Mercy there?"

She asked if it would send me running into your arms. Mercy's words from last night echoed in his head, and the rest of their conversation hit him harder than he expected. "Why would she be? I still don't understand why she's not with you."

"It's complicated."

"It always is." He hadn't meant to say that aloud and wasn't sure if he was talking about her or his current situation. He didn't know if keeping this from Liz was better or worse than telling her the truth.

"Anyway. I was abrupt last night, and I didn't want to worry you. I'm letting you know I'm okay."

"I appreciate it. Let me know if you want to talk about it." Not that he'd have any good advice. Nothing that didn't make him a hypocrite. Maybe Mercy was right; he couldn't be with her, court clients Mercy might or might not also be pursing, and watch out for Liz. And Mercy was the one variable, leaving in just a few days.

The conclusion bounced around in Ian's head as he dressed. He found Mercy on the couch. If he had to say *goodbye*, he was talking advantage of what time they had left—asking her to stay here the rest of the weekend. He also had to tell her he'd talked to Dean. It was her father, and it wasn't Ian's right to make that decision for her.

"What's up?" Her light question interrupted his rambling thoughts. "You're kind of spacing out and staring."

He shook his head, to socket all the thoughts into their individual compartments. "Admiring the view."

"Shameless flatterer." She blushed.

"And you should know, though the timing on this is bad, I don't want to keep secrets from you. I talked to Dean yesterday."

Her smile wilted. "I don't want to know about your clients."

"He called as your father. He'd like to talk to you. Asked me to give you his number, if you were interested."

"I see." She stood and grabbed her coat. "Do you have time to drop me off at the hotel before you meet Jonathan? I can call a cab otherwise."

"I'll take you." That went better than Ian expected. With any luck, the rest of the weekend would continue on a similar upward trend.

Chapter Seventeen

Mercy looked around the hotel room one last time. It *felt* empty, despite the elegant furnishings and extravagant decor. This getaway was supposed to be fun. Now her father wanted to talk to her, her best friend didn't, and her childhood crush was letting her crash at his way-too-big-for-one-person house for the rest of the weekend. Oh, and despite her resolution to stay detached, she didn't want to leave Ian behind. Not that she saw any alternative.

Her world had flipped on its head, leaving her dizzy and lost. She called Liz again—for the third time since she got back, five hours ago, and went straight to voicemail again. "You already know who this is. I'll stop stalking you, but not willingly. Please call me when you're ready to talk?"

She wouldn't check out of the room, in case Liz came back after all. A small tremor of relief settled inside that she didn't have to stay here alone, though.

Ian had messaged to say he'd be there soon. She let the door latch shut behind her and made her way to the elevator. As she stepped into the box, her phone buzzed. A string of text messages from Liz scrolled in.

If we talk, it will only be about work.
At least for now.

Not about that.

I'll take your calls. But not today.

Mercy gave a sad smile to no one in particular, and stepped into the lobby. She sent back, *I understand. Let me know?*

We'll be okay. Liz's answer came quickly. *But I need time.*

Take what you need. I'll be here, Mercy said.

Liz's reply was, *I know :)*

That was promising, right? Mercy hoped so.

Ian was waiting near the entrance when she rounded the corner. He met her halfway and took her bags. "You could have called a porter to help you."

"It felt indulgent." Some of the tension in her neck evaporated at the blandness and lack of expectation in the exchange.

He loaded her stuff into the back of his SUV, then held the passenger door open for her. "That's the point. You're staying at a high-end resort, you indulge."

"I'll keep that in mind next time. How was the snow?"

"A few days old, but still fantastic." Ian started the car and directed it toward his place. "How was the hotel cable?"

She could do small talk and meaningless banter. "Limited and distracting. Perfect combination."

"*Star Trek* marathon on Syfy?"

"Caught the tail end of it." She sank further into her seat, stress slipping from her joints. This was what she needed—to be in a different place for a little while. She wasn't sure if he knew that or was playing it by ear, but she was grateful either way. "Turned it off when wrestling started."

"What?" His question was exaggerated, laced with sarcasm and indignation. "Stories are stories."

"You're right. But sometimes a girl wants more explosions and less caveman-like chest thumping."

"There go this evening's plans. Guess we'll have to order takeout instead." He glanced sideways long enough to wink, before turning back to the road.

It felt good to laugh. "Does that Indian place still deliver? They're still around, right?"

"Yes and yes. We can stream *Star Trek* if you feel like you missed out."

The scenery passed, familiar, blanketed with white. She watched the hills roll over the top of each other, as they headed further up the mountain. "Not really. I got to see Kirk scream *Kaaaahhhhnnnn*. So I saw the best bit."

"What kind of marathon ends after two movies?" He backed the vehicle into the driveway and stopped with her door next to the front walk.

"The crappy kind," she said.

They both climbed from the car, and Ian strode to the tailgate, to grab her bags. When he shut the door, a sheet of snow slid from the edge of the roof and hit his head, before crumbling in a fine powder and settling to the ground.

"*Shit.*" He shook himself, and snow flew everywhere.

The scene, combined with the stress of the last day or so, snapped something inside Mercy. She giggled.

He looked up, brows raised. "You think that's funny?"

The fact he couldn't keep a straight face, despite his stern voice, drew her laughter out harder. "Kind of."

"Really?" He bent and vanished behind the SUV. When he reappeared, he had a handful of snow and lobbed it in her direction. "How about now?"

She squealed and ducked, reaching for a weapon of her own. When she looked up again, he was gone. "Ian?" She couldn't keep the amusement from her voice.

"Nope. Not coming out." The direction of his voice indicated he hadn't left his post.

She hid as well, straining her ears and deciding from which direction was better, to sneak up on him. She crept forward, listening, watching the shadows under the car.

"Boo." His whisper teased her cheek.

She squealed and whirled, heart leaping into her chest when she realized how close he stood.

"That wasn't for me, was it?" He grabbed her wrists and pinned them to the car, making her drop the snowball.

His heat chased the ice from her skin and drained the chill from her palms. Her laughter died in her throat when her gaze met his, and his familiar, soothing scent filled her thoughts. "Not anymore."

"Are you sure?" He dipped his head, and trailed his nose up the side of her neck, never making contact.

She sighed and tilted into him. "I'm sorry— what? I forgot all but how good that feels."

"Yeah?" He tightened his grip and kissed up her neck. "How about now?"

"That's pretty decent too."

"Maybe we should take this inside." A heavy current ran through his words and sent flames racing over her skin.

"If it were warmer, I'd let you take me outside."

He shifted his hands, so their fingers intertwined, and brushed his lips across hers. "Another thing I adore about you," he said.

Adore. How was it possible for a word to have so much power? This one spilled through her and lit her senses up as much as his touch did.

"Inside?" he asked. "Just you and me. No background. No history. Nothing but us."

That sounded like the perfect way to spend her evening. "Yes. God, yes."

*

Ian would stick to his promise. Tonight was the only point in time that existed. He used that to bulldoze any concerns about family, business, or where Mercy would and wouldn't be on Monday. How she yielded when he kissed her, her moan mixing with his growl as she leaned back against the door to close it, helped chase thought away.

He set her bags to the side, without breaking the lip-lock. He wasn't sure how he managed that, but she tasted too good—felt too right, molded against him—to let go of her for long. The smell of winter combined with her scent, and drilled into his head.

Seconds later, their coats joined her luggage, before he pressed into her again.

He needed to feel her skin. He slid a hand under her sweater, glided it up her stomach, and shoved her bra up.

She hissed and arched her back, digging into him. "Your hands are cold."

"Whose fault is that?"

Her gasps grew in speed, and she thrust against his fingers when he pinched her nipple. "Yours. I'm pretty sure." Panting punctuated her words.

"I think you're right about that." The playing was fun—the way his hard cock strained against his zipper; her squirms and sighs; the heat between them melting away the chill, even as it seeped through the door. "I think this one is getting warmer, though." He dragged his thumb over her skin, and she whimpered.

She ground into him. "I'm not sure I can hold out for a slow buildup." Her voice was strained.

"I swear you and I are on the same wavelength so often." Still massaging her breast, he moved his other hand to her waist. He popped the button on her jeans and drew down the zipper. He dipped between her legs and pushed her panties aside. Fuck, she was wet. Hot and eager.

She sucked in a sharp breath through her teeth when he trailed an icy finger over her clit.

"Too much?" He knew it wasn't, from the teeth marks she left on her bottom lip and her bumping against his touch.

She shook her head, and her hips rocked in time with the circles he traced around her sex. His dick jerked each time her clit pulsed against his skin. He wanted to be buried inside her. Her pleasure was the only thing holding his desire at bay. She moved her hands to the back of his neck and dug her nails in, the harder he rubbed. The familiar sounds of her nearing climax filled his thoughts. She cried out when she came, still shoving into his touch. As her gyrations slowed, she crushed her mouth to his, dancing her tongue in a seductive rhythm.

When she broke away, her eyes shone crystal blue and clear. Her playful, innocent smile was betrayed when she traced his shaft through his jeans and said, "Fuck me, please?"

"I love it when you talk like that." He kissed her protruding lower lip, then caught it between his teeth. "Condoms are in my room."

She nodded toward the pile of coats. "Front pocket of my purse." She broke away, and the chill that tried to rush in burned off when it hit Ian's skin.

When she bent at the waist, he studied the curve of her ass, unable to drag his gaze from the view.

She handed him the foil square, and he grabbed her hips and pulled her back into his chest. "You're so tempting." Cold and shampoo teased his senses. He trailed his hands down her arms, grasped her fingers, and raised her palms to press them against the door. It didn't matter they still wore their shoes and the rest of their clothes, his patience was gone. He dragged her jeans to her knees, and her whimpers provoked him further. It took more time than he wanted, to yank his zipper open, free his cock, and roll on the rubber.

She bent forward, teasing him with a glimpse of her glistening slit between her legs, and the last of his restraint evaporated. He gripped her hips with one hand, fisted his shaft with the other, and drove into her. She was so tight, squeezing as he glided forward. Friction built, from her legs still being together, and every time he pounded, his zipper left faint marks on her butt cheeks.

She thrust in time with him, soft whines tearing from her throat.

He sank into the stimuli, thoughts fuzzing as climax built inside. When she clenched around him, screaming with orgasm, spots swam in front of his eyes. He tried to hold back. Wanted to draw the moment out. His balls tightened, and the need for release roared in his head. He dug his fingers into her hips when he spilled inside of her, pounding until he was spent, and even then not wanting to slow.

As the frantic need ebbed, contentment seeped in, to take its place. He helped her stand and rested his forehead against her neck, still struggling to catch his breath. When she wobbled, he settled a hand on her stomach, to steady her.

"I think I need to sit." Her laugh was tired, but the stress from earlier wasn't there.

He guided her toward the couch, trying to ignore his legs' desire to give out. "Stay there. I'll get you water."

A little later, he disposed of the condom, and they cleaned up. He sat on the couch, one leg extended on the cushions, the foot of the other on the floor, and Mercy resting with her back against his chest. She pulled his arms tighter around her. Neither of them said much, but he was content to place his hand over her ribs and feel her heartbeat.

"Still want to order Indian?" Her question vanished in the crackle of the fire.

He danced his fingers over her chest. "You're not full?"

"Rein in your ego, big boy. Woman cannot survive on sex alone. I think that's biblical." She laughed.

He loved that sound. "I think you have to be bathing on the roof, and I have to be a powerful king, for this to be biblical."

She turned her head to look at him. "You've got an outdoor hot tub, right? And technically, you're the ruler of your empire. If watching's a kink…"

"I think it's safe to say at this point most things involving you are turn-ons." He snapped his mouth shut before he could make the same mistake he'd made too many times since she strolled back into his life. Swallowed his, *I wish you didn't have to go tomorrow.* He wanted to ask if she'd consider staying longer or coming back after her presentation to KaleidoMation, but he'd promised no past or future, and he wasn't going to spoil the moment.

Besides, he couldn't do that to her. It wasn't his right to ask her to uproot herself for him. "Indian food it is."

Chapter Eighteen

Mercy had gotten more good sleep this week than she remembered getting in any single block in her life, and all instances tied back to waking up next to Ian. It sucked that her work wasn't blessed with the same sense of satisfaction. She'd lost almost the entire week, and she flew out tomorrow, to pitch to KaleidoMation.

She pressed her naked body against Ian's, memorizing every inch of him as they molded together. Eyes closed, she wished the looming bitterness of having to leave didn't mar the sweetness of this moment. "We should get dressed."

"I guess." He kissed her on the forehead.

It took a force of will to step out of his grasp. They'd showered together this morning—another fantastic moment for the mental scrapbook—and the euphoria lingered on her skin. "I really have to work."

"You can use the study." He pulled clothes from drawers and dressed. "I'll give you all the space and privacy you need."

She was getting addicted to the sight of him. She dragged her gaze away and tugged on her own clothes. "Give me a few hours to wrap things up, and tonight I'm all yours."

"But just tonight."

She couldn't make herself confirm it. They both knew it was true. It had been one hell of a week, the kind of thing she'd never forget, but tomorrow morning was their expiration date. She wouldn't dwell on that. They'd do what they had up to this point, make the most of the moment, and then it would be time to move on with life.

Despite the resolution, her heart clenched and protested, making it difficult for her to cling to the words. She resisted the impulse to kiss Ian, and headed for the door instead. "I'll be downstairs."

* * * *

While Mercy worked, Ian busied himself with anything and everything. Reviewing contracts, trying to find something to watch, starting and discarding an infinite number of ideas for Thompson Advertising.

The power light blinked on his laptop, and a bubble on the screen warned he needed to find an alternate power source soon. The five or so hours his extended battery gave him weren't enough today. He hated to interrupt Mercy, but his cord was in the study. As he approached the room, he heard Mercy, and someone else drifting from the speakerphone. He focused on not listening and knocked, to draw her attention.

She looked up, and he mouthed, *Two seconds.*

She nodded. "Andr—"

"We've got some footage from spring break last year." Whoever was on the phone kept talking.

Mercy spoke again. "Hang on just a—"

"Palm Beach. Couldn't use it. Too vanilla." He kept talking, oblivious to Mercy's attempts to stop him.

"Andrew. Stop."

"What? You wanted bikinis. Right?"

Mercy rubbed her face. "Yes. But I've got other ears."

"Oh. Sorry. I'm just saying, no nipple, and enough ass coverage you should be good."

"Andrew, *stop.*" Mercy rubbed the spot between her eyes.

Despite Ian's attempts not to listen in, pieces clicked together, and a vague picture of what he heard formed in his head. If she was still working on the KaleidoMation pitch, they were discussing using her friend's porn footage for commercials.

"You can't do that on TV," Ian said.

"I loved that show when I was a kid." The voice from the phone laughed. "And yeah, you can if you do it right."

Mercy dropped her face into her hand.

"I'll let you get back to work." Ian stepped away.

"Am I keeping you from something, Merc?" The way the man said her name sounded like *Mirk*, as if she were some sort of mercenary.

Mercy gestured for Ian to stop. "Andrew, Ian. Ian, Andrew. Now everyone knows each other."

"Holy shit." Andrew's voice crackled when he raised it. "The crush? Oh, wait. I'm not supposed to say that out loud, am I?"

If this guy was an associate, Ian had a better idea where Mercy had shed a few of her inhibitions.

She rolled her eyes. "You think you're embarrassing me, but you're not. He's known longer than you have."

"And he still turned you down? Stupid bastard."

Ian didn't mind being talked about in the third person. It was kind of amusing. He did have the right to defend himself, though. "She was fifteen at the time."

"And she's not now," Andrew said. "Shit, man. Do you see her? I don't care what kind of wild-child stories she tells you about her life abroad, she's been psychologically saving herself for you for as long as I've known—"

"*Now* you're embarrassing me." Mercy talked over him. "That *off* switch I've asked you about…?"

"Jerked too hard. Broke it off."

Ian saw the pink creeping onto Mercy's face, and the clench of her jaw. This couldn't be helping her meet her deadline. As tempting as it was to distract her until she gave up, she deserved the same shot at KaleidoMation Ian had, and he'd already stolen too much of her time. "I'll let you get back to work."

"Wait." She rose enough in her seat to grab his wrist. "He knows his shit, Andrew. He does TV." She looked at Ian. "What do you mean we can't do that?"

"The censors won't let you show that much skin. I mean *no nipple*? Really? Is everything else showing? This isn't YouTube and thinly veiled context. The FCC keeps a much closer eye on network television."

Mercy shook her head. "I thought you had something new for me. The FCC also has a handful of guidelines about what is and isn't *too risqué*. We can show certain amounts of skin, as long as we cover the right bits."

"And she intends to push that line," Andrew said.

Ian should drop this. They didn't want to hear what he had to say, despite Mercy's insistence. He couldn't walk away now, though. "What happens if the censors push back?"

"We change the creative." Mercy's answer came without hesitation. "We come back with new footage that packs the same punch but subtler, and try again. It's not what I want for this market, but I'll bend if it comes down to it."

He heard the words, but they didn't make sense. "You'd waste six months of creative and push your deadlines back—what?—two to three months, in order to re-do everything, because you want to push the envelope and get risqué?"

Andrew laughed.

Ian looked at Mercy, not sure what the joke was. She said, "Six months of creative? We've pulled this together since I got into town."

"You've been pitching KaleidoMation for weeks." Ian was missing something.

"I have. And for each new round of decision making, they see something new. You do that too. Don't you?"

"Of course. But we worked it all up the moment we started bidding. We tweak each pitch based on their reactions, but we don't have time to build new story boards and art from scratch, every round of bids."

Mercy furrowed her brow. "Does Jonathan know that?"

This was getting ridiculous. "I expect he does. That's the way most companies do this. How are you not?"

"We're flexible. We don't play the *decision by committee* game."

"This isn't a matter of flexibility." Ian's frustration built that she seemed to be speaking a different language. "You're talking about shooting with new models. Assembling people out of nowhere. We don't have the budget for that kind of last-minute filming."

Mercy's mouth twitched in an unformed smile. "You don't have a business partner with terabytes of half-naked men and women in photos and video he owns the copyright to and is willing to sell."

"You're using porn?"

"*Hey.*" Andrew cut into the conversation. "Keep the disdain out of your voice. You might be immune to Miss Mercy, but you've beat your meat to videos of people fucking."

"That's not my point." Ian wasn't even sure any more what his point was.

"You've got prestige, longevity, and money behind you, Mr. Thompson." Mercy's tone shifted to calm, as if she wanted to deescalate. "I've got flexibility. That's why it's a competition, right?"

"I'll let you get back to it." Ian grabbed his charger. He wouldn't talk to two stone walls.

"Nice to finally meet you, Suit." Andrew sounded more smug than sincere.

Mercy stopped Ian halfway to the hallway and intertwined her fingers with his. "I'm almost done. Just another hour or two."

"No worries." Ian gave her a smile and strode from the room.

As he rounded the corner, he heard Andrew say, "He's protective of you. You finally fucked him, didn't you?"

Ian knew he shouldn't stop, but he couldn't help straining his ears.

"Yes." Mercy's answer was soft.

"And?" Andrew asked.

If Mercy replied, Ian couldn't hear it.

Andrew said, "I hope the reality came close to the fantasy."

"Blew everything else out of the water." Mercy sounded sad.

"I'm sorry, Merc." The brashness was gone from Andrew's voice, replaced with sympathy. "Let's wrap this up."

Ian moved out of earshot before leaning against the wall. Too many thoughts assaulted, and it all crawled under his skin, harshing his sensibility in a way he wasn't used to.

*

A few hours after the disruption, Mercy found Ian in the living room, flipping through TV channels fast enough there was no way he registered what was on. "Sorry to keep you waiting."

He dropped the remote when he turned to face her, and it clattered to the table. The smile that spread across his face was better than a hot shower on a cold day. "It's okay. Did you finish what you wanted?"

"Yeah."

"I'm sorry about interrupting."

"It's done and in the past. Nothing to worry about or apologize for." She didn't want to talk about that afternoon's conversation. They were about to be separated by several thousand miles. No reason to let work add to that chasm. "Any plans for the evening?" she asked.

"Being wherever you are." He patted the couch, and her chest squeezed in on itself.

She curled up next to him. The rest of the night passed too slowly and too fast at the same time. She didn't want to count the minutes until it ended, but her gaze drifted to the clock above the TV without her permission every few minutes.

The conversation flowed, the way it always did with Ian, hopping from one topic to the next. At some point, he suggested going to bed. It was too defining a moment, though. —like admitting their time was up. They drifted off wrapped around each other. As far as Mercy was concerned, it was worth the resulting kink in her neck the next morning.

Neither of them suggested sharing the shower this time. He let her go first, while he took care of work remotely so he could drive her to the airport. She checked in for her flight and made some last minute tweaks to travel plans while she waited for him. Then they were on their way.

Neither of them had said it yet, but she suspected he saw their goodbye looming as bleakly as she did.

"You'll keep in touch." His statement shattered her focus.

She looked at him wide-eyed, while he watched the road. He hadn't asked. It was so tempting. She'd considered it. But the chat with Andrew and Ian yesterday drove some hard points home for her. "No."

He clenched his jaw. "Just like that? You've put thought into this."

"I have."

"Care to share it with me?"

She owed him that much. "This whole thing with KaleidoMation is going to happen again, as long as we're in the same industry. Us competing, I mean. Even if we don't know up front next time, it'll come out when one of us wins the contract. Someone will be hurt." She already wondered how they'd deal with this one. Ian's refusal to back down yesterday, though she had the conversation and the project under control, was proof the friction would be there regardless of their mutual assurances.

"So business wins over lo—" Ian shook his head. "Personal relationships? I didn't realize money drove you."

The slip in words, the almost-confession, caused an internal with his implication she was doing this out of greed. "That's not fair, and that's not what this is about. I'm not asking you to give up your business; you can't expect it from me, either."

"I didn't mean that."

"I hear that from you a lot, Ian. I'm wondering when you'll say what you mean, instead of backpedaling when I call you on it."

"You want to know how I actually feel?" He gave her his full attention when they stopped for a light. "I don't want you to leave, but I can't ask you to stay. It's not fair we only got a week together. I feel selfish and childish for wanting more, but I do. I don't want to force that on you, but fuck, it'd be nice if I wasn't the only one thinking it."

"You're not"—her frustration rose, and her voice went with it—"but it doesn't matter. Even if we push everything else aside and pretend keeping in touch works, we'll be long distance. It won't last. One of us will get bored, eyes will wander, and it'll be over. I'm cutting to the chase now."

"Because it'll hurt less this way?" His tone was low and flat. Almost scarily calm. "Is that what you learned traveling? Something Andrew taught you, maybe?"

She didn't like having her past thrown back at her. A tiny voice in the back of her head said he wasn't quite doing that, but she refused to listen. "*Maybe*. Is this overbearing, possessive attitude of yours the same thing that fucked Liz up so bad?" As soon as the accusation was out, she regretted it. "Shit. I didn't mean that. She's not fucked up, and you're not overbearing."

"See how easy it is to do?" The tight cord running through his words made her think he was seconds from snapping.

She sank lower in her seat. "I'm sorry. I get it. The mind thinks things it doesn't believe, and sometimes they come out when they shouldn't."

"Yeah." He wasn't glancing at her anymore. His attention stayed fixed ahead when they stopped.

It was too late to take a new route in this conversation, but she tried anyway. "Even if we talk, and even if we never clash in business again, there's no point where one of us says, *I'll move to where you are. We'll be together.* Because when it comes down to it, this is home for you, and it's not for me." The finality of her words tasted foul, as they rolled past her lips. "I'm sorry," she said again, knowing it wouldn't change anything, but unsure what else was appropriate.

"Me too."

Chapter Nineteen

Mercy waited at the curb for the rental-car shuttle. That was one advantage to being in a state closer to California—two-hour flight instead of taking all day with layovers.

She tried not to think of other things great about Utah—like Ian. The name dragged back their less-than-happy goodbye, and she frowned. It was best this way, but it clenched like a fist around her heart, to remember the exchange.

She stepped onto the shuttle, stashed her bags on the empty spot next to her, and took out her phone. Might as well catch up with as many messages as possible in her spare minutes. She meant to pull up her email but couldn't help one more flip to the text she saw when she stepped off the plane.

Good luck.

The simple message from Ian still made her smile. She probably looked like a goof, grinning at her hand, but she couldn't help it.

There was work to do, and while the note was sweet, it was also a reminder of what she didn't have. She flipped to the email from Liz instead.

Hope this gets to you before your meeting. Call me with questions.

It was communication, and that was good. Mercy wished it was a hint friendlier, but she'd be patient. She opened a preview of Liz's attachment, and her eyes grew wide as she scanned the budget rework, complete with more money to dedicate up front to KaleidoMation.

"Miss. We're here." The driver's voice jarred her.

She shook the numbers aside enough to focus, and headed inside, to pick up her car. The moment she was on the road, headed for the hotel, she told her phone, "Call Liz." She'd made the drive enough times during the proposal process, she didn't need GPS or directions.

"Hey." Liz's cheerful greeting was a stark contrast to the tone of their recent message exchanges. "You got my email?"

"I did. You're a freaking genius. I can't believe you pulled this off. And so fast. t's you, so I can, but still."

"I'm so glad. Does this mean I can keep my job?"

Mercy laughed. This felt good. It wasn't in depth, but it was what she should have with Liz. "Hon, I'm not ever letting you leave now, if this is what I get after one weekend."

"I'm glad it's helpful. And good luck today. Not that you need it. You'll kick serious ass."

"Thanks." Mercy trailed off, not sure what to say next. If they were limited to conversations about work for the near future, it was time to say *goodbye* for now. The words stuck in her throat, and silence spilled through the car.

"I really do love you." Liz's soft comment screamed in Mercy's head.

Mercy's stomach flipped over. "Liz…"

"Not like that." The cheer was back in Liz's voice. "It's a shame we didn't get to explore that when we were younger, what with you moping over someone else and all."

The assurance was nice, but the conversation was still a reminder it was going to be a while before the two of them were back in a completely comfortable spot. "I was so terrified of me back then, it wouldn't have worked even if I wasn't pining." Over Ian. The name pinged against her ribs with an ache, and Mercy struggled to ignore it. "Don't write the whole idea off because of me. There are other women out there."

"I know. I'm not writing off anything." Liz's tone shifted to serious, almost melancholy. "I think I've wanted to explore for a while. I know I still have to deal with the whole George thing, but I don't miss him the way I expected. I feel more stupid and pissed off than heartbroken."

"He's not your fault. Sometimes you have to take a leap, and when it doesn't work out, you learn, you mourn, and then you go try something or someone new." *Do I really believe that?* Of course she did. It was her defining principle. "And in between, you eat ice cream and watch TV."

"How do you do that?"

"Do what?"

"I meant a lot of what I said the other day. I adore and look up to you, Mercy. You did something I can't. You shed your past, stopped living by everyone else's expectations, and made your own life. I don't know how to do that. I kind of hoped I might pick some of that up while you were here. I know attitude isn't an osmosis thing, and we didn't exactly have a lot of time, but…" Liz sighed.

Mercy pulled into the hotel parking lot and shut off the engine, but she didn't get out. She leaned back in her seat and stared at the ceiling of the car. "Do you want to change?" As she spoke, the question bounced in her thoughts, reflected back at her.

"It's not as easy as just saying *yes.*"

"No. It's not." Understatement of the hour. "I haven't figured it out completely." Or very much at all. "I just put up a good front." Where did this introspection come from, on Mercy's part? She dug for a source, but when she chipped away at something and her heart flinched, she backed off.

"That's not true. You've got everything together."

"You think so?" Mercy stopped a bitter laugh before it could slip out.

"I know so. I'm not pushing aside my feelings, but I've been thinking a lot. I want to experience more. Explore my sexuality. I do love you, and you're gorgeous, Mel. I mixed our friendship up with romance. But not being able to reach out to you, even for just a couple of days, made me realize I adore what we already have. And this is me being selfish, but I wish you were coming back, so we could spend more time together. Actual time, not me-hitting-on-you time."

I wish that too. The thought popped into Mercy's head, as loud as if someone screamed it.

"I'm always here by phone. Go do what you want. Freaking out is okay too, when things don't go your way. I do it all the time. Walk into some club on Saturday night, find that gorgeous guy or girl, and go home with them for the night. If you hit a panic moment, text me, and I'll remind you you're awesome. Or call the cops, depending on the situation."

"I was wrong before; you and Ian would be amazing together."

Mercy bolted upright in her seat, grabbed the phone, and tried to ignore the surge inside of something muddled. "I'm at the hotel. I have to go."

"Right. Talk to you soon." Was that disappointment in Liz's voice, or sadness?

Mercy wasn't going to linger on any of it, except that she had her friend back.

* * * *

Ian rifled through files, making sure he'd given his attention to any that needed it. Every few seconds, his gaze drifted back to the computer clock. He was fighting not to think about Mercy, and failing miserably. She'd slid into his thoughts over and over all day, and it was almost three.

She was in her meeting with KaleidoMation right now. The reminder was another reason for his back to tighten and his neck to tense. He didn't know how he wanted things to go for her. Except he did. He wanted her to succeed, and it had everything to do with who she was. Even if it meant he lost the account, he wanted her to be happy. It was a foreign feeling, and it sucked.

Not as if they'd ever see each other again. Not as lovers. Her goodbye left no room for reinterpretation, and Ian wouldn't beg for anyone's attention.

He dragged his fingers through his hair and turned his attention back to work for the infinite time that day. A new email from Jonathan Woodhouse sat in his box.

Ian's pulse stuttered, and he told himself to grow up and calm down as he clicked the message. This couldn't be a good sign for Mercy. Had they cut her off after an hour? Told her, *thanks but no thanks*?

He read.

Mr. Thompson:

I'd like to thank you again for your hospitality last week and during the entire bidding process. Thompson Advertising has a talented staff and some great offerings.

However, at this time we've decided to go a different route. Your business is strong, but we need someone more flexible. Able to adapt to a constantly shifting market at the drop of a hat.

Sincerely:

Jonathan Woodhouse

Ian's thoughts stalled on the words, and he scanned them several times, to make sure he read them right. His concern, hope, and best wishes curdled to irritation.

So Mercy wasn't done yet. She'd barely started, and they were severing ties with Ian an hour into her presentation, after Ian's company courted them for more than six fucking months. There was no way she sold them that fast.

This was why she pushed Ian away.

The moment the thought popped into his head, he hated it—*knew* it wasn't true. He couldn't shake it, though. After her insistence over the weekend that Ian wasn't flexible enough… What did she do? Open with *Unlike my competition*…

The logic centers of his brain argued, until his skull ached and screamed in protest.

He needed to bring this under control. Mercy earned the contract. He dialed her number and wasn't surprised when he went straight to voicemail. "It's Ian. I need to talk to you. Call me when you're done, even if it's late."

Shoving aside his heart, he dove straight to the truth of the matter. He owed her congratulations for a job well done.

* * * *

"One more thing, before I let you go for the evening." Jonathan's voice stopped Mercy before she could open her car door.

She spun to face him. The guy was cute. She thought so every time they met. Blond hair, dark brown eyes, and only a year or two older than she was. But he wasn't Ian—and she hated the idea the moment it squirmed into her brain. "What's up?"

Her presentation went well, as far as she knew. This guy was hard to read, so she wasn't certain, but she hit all her sales points, and the rest of the room seemed to enjoy. Afterward, Jonathan and a couple other executives took her out for an early dinner, and now she was about to head back to her hotel. It was barely seven. She might get some more work done tonight.

He rocked on his toes, and a smile crept onto a face that had been impassive most the afternoon. "I'll get you an official offer in the morning, make sure you have a current contract with all the details, but I wanted to let you know now—the contract is yours. You blew us away every step of the process."

She grinned so widely, she thought her cheeks might split. "Really?" Giddiness danced inside. "I mean, of course *really*. Why would you make that up? This is…" She forced herself to relax and shook his hand. "Thank you. We look forward to working with your entire group."

"Same." His grip was firm and warm, and his smile friendly. "Have a wonderful evening."

Joy flowed through Mercy, as she drove back to the hotel. It danced in her limbs, making her move her butt in her seat to the beat of the radio. A whisper of reality flitted in. She had nobody here to celebrate with. She could call Andrew; he deserved her *thanks*. But she wasn't in the mood for his brand of humor tonight.

She'd call Liz.

Another layer of gray settled over her cheery mood. Her win meant Ian lost. It was true, they agreed *no hard feelings*, but his team worked hard. She hoped he took the news okay. With these thoughts came a reminder he left her a cryptic message earlier. She'd wait until she was in her room, to call him back, though. And she didn't want to be the one to break this news to him. It wasn't her right, anyway. That was up to KaleidoMation.

"Ms. Rowe." The desk clerk caught her attention on the way to the elevators.

Mercy paused in front of the woman. "Yes?"

"This came in for you this afternoon. We left a message on your phone." She handed over a manila envelope.

Mercy furrowed her brows. There was nothing on it but her name. "Thanks. Have a good night." She wandered away, curious. As she stepped into a waiting car, she undid the closures and opened the flap.

Two plane tickets slid into her hand. One to Salt Lake, for tomorrow, and another back to Atlanta, two days later.

"Ian, you fucking bastard," she muttered to the empty car. Irritation battled with affection. Arrogant, presumptuous, sweet…

She snapped the thoughts off, before they headed into territory she didn't want to visit. The moment she was in her room, she dialed his number.

"I was starting to wonder if you'd call back." His greeting wasn't as warm and friendly as she expected.

She kicked off her shoes, set her purse and laptop aside, and settled onto the edge of the bed. "You said *no matter how late*. It's not even nine there." The tickets glared back at her from their spot next to the TV. How dare he?

"I thought maybe you were on an accelerated schedule. You didn't waste any time this afternoon."

His snide tone gnawed at her. What the hell? "I didn't have the luxury of having the client in my office for an entire day."

"So… you opened with *Let me tell you why my competition sucks?*"

"—the fuck?" Her voice rose in pitch, shrill to her own ears, and she forced herself to dial it back. "I don't know what you're talking about. Do you have the right number?" He apparently already knew he'd lost the contract. The realization wasn't reassuring.

"From Woodhouse, this afternoon—*We need someone more flexible. Able to adapt to a constantly shifting market at the drop of a hat.* Funny how his words echo yours."

Mercy's confusion slid back behind rage and comprehension. "You think *I* told him that?" Too many thoughts assaulted her at once. "How do you imagine it went down? I added a slide that said, *The competition? I know that guy. Dynamite in bed, but a little stiff when it comes to change. You want flexible? I'm your woman.*"

"You did something."

She refused to acknowledge the ache in her joints. The hurt throbbing through her veins, at what his accusations meant. "I sold my fucking product. That's what you did, that's what I do. Whatever conclusions they drew—correctly, I'll add—about your inability to adapt, were probably because they're fucking observant. I suppose now that you're pissed at me, you want back these plane tickets I never asked for?"

"I didn't buy you any tickets." His voice shifted from irritated to a scarily low calm, with a heavy current running through it. "You made it clear we're done. Do you really think that little of me?"

"I think you run your company like an uptight old man." She was done holding back. "And speaking of how we feel about each other, do you think I'd compromise my ethics for a little bit of an upper hand? Is your opinion of my work so fucking low, that you believe I have to do that? Was all of that *I'm impressed with what you've done* just lip service?" Her last question echoed through the room.

Someone pounded on the wall next door and shouted, "*Shut up.*"

"No. That's not what this is about," Ian said.

"You could have fooled me." Mercy lowered her voice but couldn't ignore the storm inside her. "I usually don't get much satisfaction out of saying something like this, but tonight I will. Long distance doesn't work. Competing for the same clients doesn't work. *I told you so.*"

"Fantastic." His sarcasm matched her irritation. "Too bad that doesn't keep anyone warm at night."

"No. But rage is a nice substitute." She disconnected before he could say anything else. The last thing she needed was to hear more of his excuses. Another thinly veiled attempt to backpedal and pretend this wasn't a big deal. *Fucking asshole.*

She rolled onto her side, pulled her knees to her chest, and did something she hadn't since that first stranger in Venezuela. She cried over a man.

Chapter Twenty

Ian wanted to throw his phone at the wall. Instead he settled for screaming, *"Fuck,"* in the empty house. As soon as he'd said the words, the moment he accused Mercy of playing dirty, he knew he was wrong. It would have been nice if he figured that out sooner. Almost as good if pride let him take his accusation back, instead of digging the pit deeper.

He had to make this right. Tell her he didn't feel that way. She deserved to be treated better. The moment his frustration ebbed enough he could think straight, he called her back. It went to voicemail. "Mercy, I'm sorry. I know that doesn't make what I said right, but let me try?"

He leaned back against the sofa with an *oomf* and tried to keep his mind from scattering again. She'd been gone half a day after being back in his life for a week. He already missed her so much it hurt, *and* had offended her in one of the worst ways he could imagine. Liz was right; he was bad for Mercy.

His next message was a text. *Hear me out?*

He wouldn't beg. He didn't grovel. *Fuck.* This was his fault. She kept him at a distance, but that didn't make her underhanded or manipulative. As far as he knew, she'd always been upfront with him.

You don't have to call me back. Just know, I'm so sorry.

He didn't know what else to do.

* * * *

Mercy ignored every ring and chime from her phone. The first call was Ian, and she deleted his message without listening. She wasn't interested in seeing who the rest belonged to.

Would it be worse or better if he only tried the once?

Long after the tears dried up and the numbness settled in, she forced herself from the bed and crossed the short distance to where the plane tickets sat, taunting her. When she picked up the envelope, a note fluttered to the ground. She shouldn't read it. She needed to tear it up along with the gift, and forget she ever knew Ian, He said they weren't from him, but she had a hard time trusting anything he'd said right now.

She couldn't help herself.

Melissa,

I was hoping to see you while you were here. If you have time, I'd love to have lunch with you and maybe start to make things right. The home number hasn't changed. Call us if you're interested.

Love,

Dad

Her tears spilled out, and an empty pit grew inside, threatening to consume her, as she sank to the floor.

Sleep didn't come that night. She teeter-tottered between trying not to think about Ian, being furious with him, and wondering why she was considering using the tickets from her father. It was a chance to see Liz again, but Mercy couldn't use a gift like this and not see the giver.

Why would she want to? Her family had never been anything but dismissive. Her two brothers and one of her sisters turned their backs on her when she left, but not before reminding her this was the kind of thing people burned in hell for.

Did Dad really want to make amends, or was this an excuse to lecture her about how badly he thought she screwed up her life? She shouldn't care. But she did. Her home life as a kid was never abusive. Strict, intolerable, and suffocating, but it came from a place of love—misguided, but still love.

Mercy was tired of being alone. She had Liz and Andrew, and they were all but family, so why wasn't that enough?

The thoughts were cyclical, haunting her until the sky peeking through the top of her curtains shifted from black to gray. It was after seven, back home. She wasn't concerned she'd wake the household. *Home.* The thought made her snort. It hadn't been home for ages.

She dialed her dad's number from memory, heart slamming against her ribs with every ring.

"Hello?" A chipper female voice answered.

Mercy swallowed, struggling to find her voice. "Susan?"

"Oh, my heck. Mercy?" Her youngest sister, Susan—who was twenty now if Mercy's math was good—was the only sibling who ever used her preferred name.

A smile cracked onto Mercy's face. "It's me. Is Dad there?" It felt so foreign saying the words, and Mercy couldn't keep the timidness from leaking into her question.

"He had to go to work early. You just missed him." Susan sounded painfully cheerful. "But he said, if you called, to tell you he'd drop everything for lunch. Are you coming back?"

"He's not going to drop *everything* for me." Despite the argument, a ball of warmth spread through the knot in Mercy's chest.

"I promise he will. Is that a *yes*? Is this your cell number? What time will you be here?"

The attitude was contagious. "Plane doesn't get in until eleven, so probably not until after one. That's a little late for lunch."

"Doesn't matter. *Yay*, I'm so super psyched to see you!"

"Give me your cell, and I'll text you when I get in." Mercy scribbled the digits, to add to her phone as soon as they disconnected. Her gut churned, and her nerves marched quadruple time. She was going to do this. She prayed it wasn't a huge mistake.

The next few hours passed in the most agonizingly slow blur she'd ever lived.

At the boarding gate, she texted Liz. *I'll be in town tonight, after all. Do you have time?*

Liz's answer came back within seconds. *Always.*

Followed quickly by, *Wait. Maybe. Back in town why? To see Ian?*

His name left a lump in Mercy's throat she couldn't swallow past. There was too much to say in a few short words, so she decided to ignore the question. *Why maybe? Are we not there?*

It's not like that. But plans change, you know?

Mercy smiled and managed to push down the ache Ian's name carried. *Is this a living life for the moment kind of thing?*

Something like that. Tell me when and where, and you'll know if plans change.

Mercy frowned at the odd phrasing but couldn't figure out why it felt off. Still, seeing Liz again would be fantastic. Her mood lifted another notch. She boarded the plane when they called her row number, and she settled into the business-class seat.

When the plane took off, the butterflies inside soared, while the rest of her stomach lurched. She recognized the feeling. It settled in every time she hopped on a flight to wherever she called *home* at the time. A nervous anticipation that rolled under her skin and pumped her with adrenaline.

Today it was amplified tenfold, and she was just visiting the damned place. She pulled up some work, but it didn't hold her attention. Tried to read but couldn't focus. The games on her phone failed to distract her. Her gaze kept drifting out the window, to the mountains and desert below. She tried to guess where they were, based on how much time passed. Was that St. George? The little town nestled in the hills had to be Cedar City, right?

And then the nervousness spiked. She knew Provo. The flight attendant announced they began their final descent. About forty minutes, and she'd be on the ground. The snow-covered mountains rose and then fell away, revealing the next valley over. She tapped her fingers on her leg. The nervousness hadn't been this severe in... She didn't know how long. This felt like coming home more than any place she'd ever been, including Atlanta.

She missed it here. The realization slammed her in the gut, making her shake. Despite trying to run from it for so long, denying that she ever wanted to be here again, it really was home. Liz was here. If she was lucky, Susan and maybe more of her family was here.

And, as much as she hated to admit it, she adored that Ian was here too. God, she missed him. Not as the little girl with ideals and stars in her eyes, but as his equal, opposite, challenger, lover... More. His words from last night still hurt, though. The assumptions he jumped to yesterday were proof he didn't see her the same way. Could she reconcile that? Could she forgive him? She knew better than to get attached to someone she was fucking. Why did she let herself get sucked into the fairytale?

She stashed thoughts of Ian behind happier things. When she touched down, she grabbed a shuttle to take her up the mountain, and texted Susan that she was on her way. Liz was staying down here, so Mercy would get an airport hotel room when lunch was over, and spend the rest of her time in town working and catching up with her best friend.

The ride into Park City was gorgeous, as Mercy expected. Snow glinted in the sunlight, and the mountains flowed into each other. Her attempts at being calm failed when she stepped out in front of the restaurant. Would they be waiting for her inside? God. Was she really doing this?

She passed through the front door and heard a squeal from the far end of the trendy bistro.

"*Mercy.*" Susan pushed back from the table where she sat with their dad, and half skipped to meet her. Her sister could have been her twin, except her hair barely reached her ears and had a bright blue streak running through it. Her fitted T-shirt read, *Screw the Establishment.*

The substituted cuss word tickled Mercy's amusement. Leave it to this town to take a rebellious message and jerk the steam out of it. "Hey," Mercy said.

Susan threw her arms around Mercy's neck. Mercy was startled but returned the tight hug. Her family was never touchy-feely. This was new.

"I'm so glad you're here." Susan grabbed her hand and tugged her toward their dad.

He stood as they approached, gave her a thin lipped smile, and took his seat again when they did.

That was the dad Mercy remembered.

"I'm glad you came." His tone was stern and even. Like the last time she saw him.

Any peace she found on the ride up the mountains vanished, and her muscles clenched. "Of course." What else was she supposed to say?

"I wanted to do this in person." His voice shifted, and he studied his hands, clasped on the table. "I'm sorry for what I said the other day, and that it's been so long since we've spoken. I'm sorry for a lot of things."

Mercy's brain ground to a halt, as she fumbled over the sincerity in his gaze. She had so many options right now—stand up and walk out; tell him it was too late; drag him over the coals until he groveled. Only one answer felt right, though. "Me too. To all of the above."

"So, I… uh—" He cleared his throat. "I'd like to figure out how to have you back in our lives. No stipulations. No expectations. I can't say I understand why you did what you did, but if it's made you happy…"

"It really has."

He smiled. "I'd love to hear about it, if there's a PG-rated version."

The warmth Mercy felt the night before rushed back. "There is. I promise."

It all felt right, except the one missing piece. That one chunk with Ian's name and all the hurt he managed to inflict with a few words. If she stayed in the valley her odds of bumping into him were low. Damn it, how long would it take to get over him?

Chapter Twenty-One

I think you run your company like an uptight old man.

Mercy's accusations—realities?—from last night hadn't left Ian alone.

Whatever conclusions they drew about your inability to adapt were because they're observant.

Every time he let his mind wander, they popped in for a visit.

Is your opinion of my work so fucking low that you believe I have to do that?

He fucked up. His family's agency had been crumbling when he took over, and he saved it. If he wasn't willing to explore other options now, it wouldn't stay that way.

Thinking about Mercy led to frustration and regret, so he tried to focus on KaleidoMation's feedback about flexibility instead. That led back to her. She hadn't answered his messages. Was probably screening his calls…

You want these plane tickets back that I never asked for?

The new sentence popped into his head without warning. What plane tickets? No. He had work to do, and that included his 2 PM with his sales team.

He filed Mercy as far out of reach as he could, grabbed his notebook, and headed into the conference room.

Jake, was already waiting, and the rest of the group filed in over the next couple of minutes. Always on time. Every one of them.

A week ago, their punctuality made him bristle with pride. Now it nagged at him. Was he over-thinking this *no flexibility* thing? Maybe a little.

Perfect time to meet about it. He almost rolled his eyes at his sarcasm. This was a good start to a solution, though. He hired these people out of college, for their fresh grasp and outlook on the market. They might be a little stalled in their methods now, but they could move past it.

He took his spot in front of the room, whiteboard marker in hand. "Today's meeting is about flexibility. We need it. How do we get it?"

Suggestions flew at him for the next hour. Each required as much red tape as the last. Why did everything in his company have to touch so many people on its journey?

"Why?" Ian asked. "Why does it have to go to committee next?"

Jake furrowed his brow, as if it were the dumbest question he'd ever heard. "That's how the process works. Concept. Committee approval. Design. Committee approval. Present internally. Committee approval."

"But why?" Ian asked again.

"Because that's the way we've always done it," someone else said.

The phrase taunted Ian and dragged him back to when he took over. He'd laid people off for telling him the same thing. And then he brought in this group to innovate… and made them follow the rules. The realization struck him hard. "What if we changed procedure? Or threw it out the window? If it was an option to go directly to the client with your concept, would you?"

"Why would I do that?" someone else asked. "What if the client hates it?"

"What if they hate it anyway?" Fuck. Mercy was so right; he was entrenched in bureaucracy.

Jake pushed aside his laptop. "Then at least everyone else signed off first, so we can tell the client the idea tested well."

"So this is a share-the-blame kind of thing?" Ian couldn't believe it. That's what he'd cultivated.

"No." Jake didn't look like he believed his own words.

This was getting them nowhere. Ian hid his frustration. "Time's up. We'll do this again in a week. Think about this from every other angle possible before then."

Liz was waiting in his office when he returned. That was a bright spot in his day.

"I hope you didn't wait long," he said as he dropped into his chair, across the desk from her.

"Nope. Jake told me when you had a break. What are you doing for dinner tonight?"

That sounded like a perfect distraction for the evening, as long as he didn't ask Liz about work. Or Mercy. Or… *Fuck.* "I'm free."

"Perfect." She fiddled with her fingers, watching them dance off each other.

"There's more."

"There is. I have to give a deposition about George, to keep the process going, and I know it's kind of childish of me to ask, but"—sadness tinged her voice—"will you go with me?"

This was right. The way it should be. He and Liz looked out for each other. "Yeah. Of course."

"Thank you." She smiled but still didn't meet his gaze. What was she up to? She looked up. "You haven't asked yet."

Asked… He dragged through all the possible things he might want to know and ticked each off the list as something she couldn't or wouldn't tell him.

You want these plane tickets back that I never asked for?

There was no way. "Is Mercy in town?"

"Yes. And you should call her."

"I've tried that." He didn't want to get into details. Not with Liz or anyone. He'd been a Grade-A jackass, and that was a hard thing to admit to himself, let alone out loud.

"But you're free tonight."

"I'm having dinner with you." As he spoke, he realized what she'd asked. "That's not why you wanted to know."

A mischievous smile played on Liz's face. "I'll tell you where I'm meeting her, and you'll take my place."

"No. Definitely not. If she's pissed at me now, something tells me that will make her furious."

"Why?" She leaned in and rested her arms on the desk. "I've never seen either of you smile as much as you did over the last week. What in the entire universe could make that a bad thing?"

"You don't know what I said to her."

"You screwed up?"

"So badly." A weight lifted from his chest. It left a gaping crater in its place, but at least the pain was new.

Liz raised her brows.

"What?" Ian asked.

"In my life—like, the whole freaking thing—I've never once heard you say you were wrong."

She was exaggerating. Had to be. He wasn't like that. "That's not true."

"It is."

Confession was nice, but it didn't bring solutions. He wanted a new subject. "Why are you so insistent? How can you be so optimistic about love in general, when—" He stopped himself before he could say too much. Even when Mercy wasn't here, he was speaking his mind before he thought.

"When I've lost it twice?" Liz completed the thought exactly as it sat on the tip of his tongue. "When I wanted it so badly I let bad judgement almost drive me into marrying a man who only wanted me for my money the second time, despite your insistence I be cautious? It makes me want it even more, because I know it's out there. I've tasted it. I'm addicted to it. I want the same thing for the people I love."

"What if she and I break each other?"

She gave a sad chuckle. "Mercy told you I said that?"

He shrugged, unsure what to say that didn't involve spilling more of him than he cared to.

"Then you enjoy the ride while it lasts. The two of you don't usually hide from risk. Does the fact that this scares you tell you anything?"

"I'm not scared. Mercy isn't talking to me."

"Yeah. Okay." As she stood, she slid a piece of paper across the desk. "You've always been there for me. Let me look out for you, this once."

"That's not what this is." He almost said, *you don't understand.* But then she'd ask him to explain, and he didn't get it either.

"That's what this is. I'm saving the two of you from yourselves. This is the last time I'll nudge, and then you're on your own. Don't fuck it up again."

After she left, Ian stared at her scrawl for several minutes. A restaurant in Salt Lake and a time.

Go or not?

* * * *

Mercy shifted her weight from one foot to the other, to keep warm. She got to the restaurant early but wasn't in the mood to sit inside alone. That meant standing on a downtown street, as the temps dropped below freezing, and wondering if she'd stopped feeling her toes because it was cold or because she'd stomped her feet one too many times.

Her phone buzzed in her purse, and she fumbled for it. It wouldn't be Ian; he'd stopped messaging her. And she was still grateful she hadn't read a single one. The thought didn't make her as happy as she wanted.

Liz's note read, *Forgive me?*

Weird. *For what?*

For giving Dean your hotel information. For… other things. Tell me I'm forgiven?

Mercy stared at the messages. This explained how the plane tickets made it to her. She would have blown a gasket if Liz told her before the fact, but Mercy was so grateful now that the meeting took place. She sent a reply. *Probably always. What other things?*

"You're early." Ian's voice settled into Mercy's head, drilled through her body, and danced in her gut.

I'm going to kill you, she sent to Liz.

I love you too.

"Am I interrupting?" Ian sounded more amused than annoyed.

She looked up from her phone. That was a mistake. He looked as incredible as ever, in jeans and a sweatshirt, with a leather coat over it all. Delicious, delectable, and attached to everything bad that happened over the last twenty-four hours. She was too tired for this shit. "Yes. I'm plotting your sister's murder. Come back never."

He stepped aside when she brushed past him. "I don't have a right to ask, but hear me out?"

His request stalled her. The answer was *no*. It hovered on the tip of her tongue. She turned back to face him. "I'll listen, but it won't change my mind." She couldn't bend on this. Gorgeous, fun, brilliant— none of it mattered if he didn't respect her. If she didn't cling to that thought for all she was worth, she'd regret it.

"I'll take that." He nodded toward the micro-brewery. "Do you want to go inside? It's warmer."

She *wanted* to forget he'd hurt her, find a dark corner, and let him heat her up.

That wasn't an option. She nodded. "Inside sounds good."

Chapter Twenty-Two

The hostess showed them to a table near the window, with a less-than-stellar view of the brick wall next door. Ian wouldn't have felt differently about the scenery if their seats overlooked a masterpiece of glory and nature. He was only looking one place.

Cheeks flushed from the cold, Mercy sat across from him, rubbing her fingers together and studying the drink menu with an intensity he wished was on him. When she'd turned away outside, Ian was worried she wouldn't stop.

"Can I start you folks off with something to drink?" the waitress asked. According to her nametag, she was Greta.

"Water for me." Ian wanted a clear head for this—or as clear as was possible, with Mercy around.

Mercy gave the girl a thin smile. "Greyhound for me."

She was going straight for the hard liquor. That wasn't good.

"Appetizer to go with that?" Greta tapped her pen on her pad. "I can't serve you the drink unless you order food. And I need to see your ID."

Mercy muttered something under her breath about stupid Utah drinking laws, and pulled out her driver's license. "Chips and salsa, then."

"Sure. Be right back."

Mercy took her time putting her purse away, adjusting her phone in its pocket several times before letting the bag dangle from its strap on the back of her chair. She drummed her fingers on the table, shrugged out of her coat—that had to be a good sign, right?—and fiddled with the edge of the menu. She still wouldn't look at him. "You wanted to talk?" Her tone wasn't as icy as the air outside, but it was close.

There was so much to tell her. How amazing she looked. How much he missed her, though it had been less than two days since he saw her last. How intensely he wanted to give *them* a try. That all needed to wait. Apologizing was the priority, and he was prepared to grovel. Earning back the trust he destroyed with his careless words.

He sifted through his jumbled thoughts and tugged at one. "I'm not very good at this, and the thing about being around you is I say things without thinking…" Even before she scowled, he knew that wasn't the right starting point.

"So this is my fault?" She pursed her lips.

"No. That's not it."

"The thing is you're thinking it." A current of exhaustion ran through her words. "That's why you say it. What you're not doing is filtering it. And I don't want you to. I'd rather know up front you think poorly of my business prowess, than have you hide it."

"I don't think poorly of your work." He'd dug himself an epic hole.

"Really? Your track record and actions imply otherwise."

Time to stop hedging and start laying this all out. "I think the world of you, Mercy"—she raised her brows, and he continued before she could cut him off—"but I also think pretty highly of myself."

The corners of her mouth twitched, as if she was fighting a smile, and a small laugh slipped out.

"I love that sound," he said.

"This ranks pretty low on the list, as far as apologies go. As in, I'm not hearing one in the middle of all of this. Now, it's true you're up against some winners, and the competition is tough. Andrew's a master of *I'm sorry.*"

Of course he was competing with the porn guy. He wasn't jealous, but it did sting a little. "But you're not with him, so he can't be that good."

"He's not you." She sighed. "And you being you doesn't matter either, if the conversation keeps going in this direction."

Now would be the wrong time to call her on how convoluted that was. "Does that mean I still have a chance to make things right?" he asked.

"I'm here." She held up a finger, silencing him when he tried to speak. "But no more bullshit about how I make you say things you don't want to. I want the unfiltered you."

So much of what she said over the past week or so clicked into a complete image for Ian. Somewhere along the way, when Mercy was learning to be herself, he was forgetting and becoming what everyone else wanted instead. The revelation confirmed that his plan, the one big thing he wanted to do tonight besides apologize, was the right decision. He hoped she agreed. "Here's the real, unfiltered truth. Though I've had a day to think about it, so it's got some introspection behind it… and an intense desire for you."

Greta returned with their drinks, but Mercy ignored hers. She nibbled on a chip instead.

"You ready to order?" Greta asked.

Ian looked at Mercy, who shook her head. He turned back to Greta. "Maybe some potato skins."

Mercy ducked her head, but not before he saw her smile. "You remembered," she said.

"You sound surprised. You never ordered anything else back then."

Her smile grew. "Anyway, introspection helps us grow. It's part of the learning process."

"When did you figure all of this out?"

"You taught me."

He didn't remember doing that. "I'm a smart guy. I'm glad you listened." He winked and put a laugh in his words. "I'm also sorry. So very, very sorry. It's not that I think you don't deserve the contract. You do. I know you earned it. I just couldn't fathom that I'd done something to lose it, and I took that out on you…" He had more to say, but admitting guilt was hard enough. The next step terrified him.

"There's more, isn't there?"

Why did she have to read him so well? He tried to pull up the words, but instead got, "Does there have to be?"

"No. I'd take your apology as it stands; I don't like hating you. But I can tell you have more to say."

"I want a partnership." There. That wasn't so hard.

Except she was looking at him, brow furrowed, as if he spoke Swahili. "Is that some trendy-business-guy way of… You know what? I don't know what you're asking, and I'm not going to guess."

"I'm talking about a business merger. Thompson Advertising and Graceful Exhibition Advertising."

"Is that code for *you buy me out, use my name as a secondary brand, and beat everything unique out of it while you lay off the handful of staff I have?*"

She thought he'd do that? To anyone? He didn't have a right to be offended, after what he accused her of. "I'm talking about being equal partners. Not me running things or buying anyone out. An actual merger. What you were talking about with Andrew? How quickly you can move and act on things? I want that for Thompson Advertising. The company needs it. And I'm hoping you feel like I bring something to the table too. This gives you access to a bigger budget and a new client list."

"You're not the only one with established contacts. It also gives you access to my list. Convenient."

He was saying something wrong. "It does. I want this to be a mutually beneficial partnership."

"Is this a way to get Liz back under your wing and working for you?"

"This is a way to get you working by my side. Not *for* me. Not answering to anyone. Why are you struggling with that?" He didn't mean to let the irritation leak into his voice, but he couldn't stop it.

"Life doesn't work that way. Thompson Advertising is huge. Companies like yours don't bow down to teensy little guys like me and say, *please teach us.*"

"Companies like *them,*" he said. "We need to adapt and change. I don't want to think the way *companies like them* do. That's why I'm making this offer. If we don't have something you think would benefit you, tell me *no.* Bottom line is I can't compete with you. Not because of the whole attraction thing, though that makes it difficult, but because you've got me beat, innovation-wise. I don't want to be the other guy again, because competing with you terrifies me." It felt odd to say it, but he knew she wouldn't throw it in his face.

*

Despite Mercy's attempt to keep a cool front, Ian's offer floored her. When she agreed to stay, she expected a few pretty words, and she hoped to be moved enough to work things out and find some sort of common ground.

This, though… It tweaked her mind and obliterated her plausibility censors. Every instinct she had told her it was bullshit. She was tired of her cynical outlook. She wanted Ian's offer to be real, for so many reasons. The business benefits were only one. She was ready to accept his apology before he made the offer, though she'd have doubted him for a long time. Pushed harder than she should, to make him prove it day after day. Now she knew he was sincere.

It didn't mean she had to be stupid about the whole thing. "If I say *yes*, we'll need to discuss details. We're doing this by the book." She dug into the food and ignored her drink. She thought the liquor would take the edge off, but Ian did a good job by himself.

"Really? Red tape and all?" He sounded amused but not surprised.

"Some things don't get left to chance. There are other parties involved with this. I take care of my people. I want to see the contracts. We'll both undergo due diligence. My lawyer will review *everything*."

He shook his head, smile growing. "You always amaze me."

"You thought I'd go into this blindly?"

"This is a work in progress for me. I didn't think past how to get you on my side without stifling what makes you unique or taking away from your company. I don't want you working for me or consulting or anything like that. This doesn't work unless we're equal partners."

Damn it—why did he have to be all reasonable and complimentary? "Let's put the whole thing in motion. No promises. Maybe you don't have what I need, but I'm hoping you do."

He traced his toe up her shin. "Me too."

A yawn forced its way out, threatening to split her jaw. It had been a long few days.

Ian raised his brows. "Am I boring you?"

"No. Exactly the opposite." The peace that evaded her last night settled in now. She felt comfortable and content. "But I haven't slept since… Umm…" Her foggy thoughts resisted her attempt to find information. "Well, Saturday we screwed half the night. Sunday, we slept on the couch and not a lot, and Monday…"

"What about it?"

"I stayed up all night, hating you."

Chapter Twenty-Three

Hating you. The words hit Ian harder than he thought possible, wrenching everything inside. "I'm sorry. Flowery words and rambling aside, I really am. My merger offer is independent of my apology, and something I know will take time—and that's only if you agree. But both are sincere. Completely and honestly."

"I know. And I mean it that I'll look at everything. One of us has to be a rational adult about this." A teasing glint tugged up the corners of her eyes.

He was going to push his luck a little harder. "So… losing sleep over me. That means I'm not the only one hooked."

"No comment." Her growing amusement was broken by another yawn.

"You need your rest. Do you want to get out of here?"

"I'm good…" Another yawn. "Or maybe not so much."

He tossed some money on the table. "Did you drive? Are you okay to make it back to your hotel?"

"I caught a cab."

"Come on." He took her belongings from the back of her seat, nudged her to stand, and helped her shrug her coat on. "I'll take you back. Where are you staying?"

"Airport Super 8." She laughed.

"Did I miss something?"

"No." She slid her hand into his. Despite the chill on her still-cold fingers, a jolt of heat raced through him. His pulse sped another notch when she leaned her head on his shoulder as they headed outside. "I was thinking… I used to wonder what it would be like to have someone dote on me the way you do on Liz." Her voice was tired.

He didn't know how he missed that before. "I don't *dote*."

"Whatever. You do."

He wasn't in the mood to argue, even over something small. "And that's funny?"

"No." She leaned more of her weight against him. "But now I know how it feels. It's pretty fucking nice."

Letting go of her so she could hop into the SUV made him itch for her touch. He was addicted. She didn't let go of his hand yet. She kept her legs dangling outside the car and tugged him to stand between them. "I have a favor to ask." The bravado vanished from her voice.

"Of course. Anything. You have to know that."

"I assumed you'd say that, but don't promise me the world yet."

He was willing to. The thought hit him hard and rocketed from his hair to his toes. He wasn't sure what to do with the information. "What is it?"

"Stay with me tonight?" She studied him through her lashes. Fuck. She wore *demure* as well as she did everything else.

"You need your sleep," he said.

"And I'll get it." She tugged him closer and rested her forehead on his chest, muffling her words. Her hot breath seeped through his shirt and teased his skin. "That's why it's a selfish request. I won't be very good company."

He kissed the top of her head, drawing the moment in his mind and sealing it there. "Of course I will. Always."

* * * *

Mercy leaned into Ian, as he glided his lips down the back of her neck. God. He was good at that.

"I have to go into the office." His words vibrated against her skin.

It was barely six. She didn't realize people got up this early and stayed sane—except Liz.

Mercy felt better than she had in ages. Even weirder, after expecting to be up half the night despite her exhaustion, she'd passed out by nine. It turned out that having Ian there—not fighting how much she liked him; the peace that came from lying in his arms—was rather relaxing.

She tilted her head, to give him a better angle. "If you were the boss, maybe you could make your own hours."

"These *are* my hours." He kissed along her shoulder and trailed his fingers down her arm. "Are you going to be gone and vanished into the deep recesses of another state, before my work day is over?" His voice hitched at the end of the question.

She wasn't going back. The thought was there since she touched down yesterday, and niggled at her even before then. She wasn't sure she was ready to tell him that yet. "My ticket is for Thursday afternoon."

"Another day." He gripped her hip "Leave room for me in your schedule. I want to see you tonight." He pressed closer, as if to emphasize his point, and his hard length teased her.

"You don't want to see me right now?" Uncertainty loomed, but much of the stress was behind her. It left room for a playful spark inside. She shifted enough to roll onto her back, so she could see him. She inched up the bottom of her shirt, but stopped when it was halfway up her ribs.

He groaned and settled his palm on her stomach. "I have to work."

"So you'd leave me here all alone?" She pulled off her top and tossed it aside. "Naked and unsupervised?"

"Only for the day. I'll be back tonight." In a single motion, he shifted his weight enough to hold her in place and pinned her hands above her head. He scraped his teeth along her collarbone.

She squirmed underneath him, not to get free, but because the friction danced along her skin, lighting her senses on fire. "But that's so *long*." She stretched out the word and rubbed her hip against his cock. Her panties and his boxers didn't provide much of a barrier. "It'll be so *hard* to wait."

"You should have thought of that before you started undressing." He blew across one nipple, never making contact, and it hardened to a nub.

Dampness grew between her legs, which slipped and slid each time she shifted position. "You've got five minutes, right? It's still early."

"If you get me started, I'm not going to want to walk away."

"We're already started."

"How about this, then? I want to take my time with you. Five minutes is a joke."

She worked one hand free and grabbed him through his shorts. She stroked his length, languishing in the chills his moans sent through her. "Big words, big guy. Do you have the stamina to back it up?" She'd let him leave, but he didn't seem more interested in doing so than she was in watching him go.

He knelt, and let go of her hand, as he wedged one knee between her legs. "Is that a challenge?"

"I don't know. I'd hate to keep you from work."

He cupped one of her breasts and grazed his thumb over the rigid peak. She twisted against the rough contact, whimpering for more.

"Still want me to leave?" His voice rolled deep and low through her body.

"I'm pretty sure I was the one who wanted you to stay a little longer…" She sighed when he lowered his head and flicked his tongue over her other nipple.

He nipped at the sensitive skin with his teeth, then alternated between sucking and licking. Need spiraled through her, traveling to her gut and pooling between her legs. She writhed beneath him, trying to draw closer one moment and wriggling to get away the next, when he hit the right nerves and pleasure spiked through her. She wasn't sure how long he spent alternating between her breasts, lavishing them with attention. Her head grew light, and she shifted closer to the leg just out of reach of her aching core.

When she thought he couldn't take it anymore, he pulled away. Disbelief and cold air spilled over her but didn't cool the heat begging for more.

She grabbed his hand when he tried to rise from the bed. "Wait." It was a struggle to force the word through her dry throat. "Where are you going?"

"Condom."

"I don't care." The frantic desire inside wasn't willing to wait the few seconds this conversation took. "IUD. I'm safe."

"Me too."

"Forget it, then."

As he drew his mouth along her collarbone, up her jaw, and to her lips, he murmured, "And here I thought you couldn't get sexier."

"You're biased." She arched her back at each feather-light kiss and caress.

"Yup." He stripped off her panties, knelt between her legs again, and supported his weight with one hand near her head. He fisted his cock and dragged the head along her slit. "Fuck, you're soaked."

The teasing made it hard to think, especially when he bumped her clit. She thrust, to get closer, and he drew away, dipping near her opening before sliding back up.

She couldn't find a response. "More?"

"You'll have to be specific." He bumped her throbbing button again but didn't move away. When he pumped his hand, stroking his cock, he hit her clit at a delicious angle.

She gripped the sheets, clenching her hands until her knuckles ached, focused on the pressure building inside. "That's good."

"Like this?" He rubbed faster, jerking them both off at the same time.

She nodded, not trusting herself to speak. Orgasm built inside, slow and steady, nudging her closer to the edge with each bump. As he increased his speed, she struggled to catch her breath.

When she peaked, climax tearing through her, he pushed inside with a hard thrust.

Being stretched out as she came, feeling him hammer the right spot, drew out her pleasure. One moment faded into the next, and she lost herself in the bliss rolling through her.

There was no way she could walk away from this. From him. And it wasn't just how in sync they were in bed—though that helped.

He kissed her hard, still slamming against her, steadily and with hungry intensity. The kiss filled her with all the pleasantness since they found each other again. Each moment of joy, laugh, and exquisite thrill.

She definitely couldn't give him up.

Chapter Twenty-Seven

Ian clenched his jaw, to keep from coming too soon. He wanted this to stretch forever. Or at least, as long as possible. This wasn't an intense lust-fueled fuckfest, like they shared in the past. Though it was fierce, this was making love. *Wow.* He really did love her. The parting of her lips, as she drew close to climax again. Her hair fanned around her on the pillow. That he was late for work, and he'd still stick around to talk, enjoying every minute of it.

"God, Ian." Even the way she gasped his name sent tendrils of pleasure snaking through him. She arched her back under him, wrists straining against his grip, but not to get away. "You feel so amazing."

She tightened around him when she came, clenching, teasing, and grinding against him. He pounded harder, falling into the ecstasy, thoughts turning to vapor, until all that remained was him and her. His grunts melded to a single groan when he spilled inside her. He still didn't want to stop, but as release flowed through him, the frantic thrusting ebbed and faded. He rested his hands on both sides of her head and kissed her, before leaning his forehead against hers. "Fuck, you're beautiful."

"Shameless flatterer." She smiled and nudged him, prompting him to roll onto his side, so he could still see her.

He couldn't let her get away. It would suck, sending her back home tomorrow. Again. But he needed something more from her than *long distance doesn't work*. "I mean every word of it. I also mean it when I say I love you."

"I—" She caught her bottom lip between her teeth, and pulled her gaze from his. "You need to get to the office, not run my company into the ground before I get to it."

Not the response he hoped for, but he wasn't done yet. The hint of numbness spreading through him was misplaced. He'd rather feel this than block it out, even if things between them ended up not working. They would go the way he wanted though. "Soon. First, though, I know you keep telling me it won't work, but I'm stubborn."

"You? Nah." She gave a short laugh.

He kissed the tip of her nose. "I'm going to ask one more time—reconsider trying things out, long distance. I'm not ready to give up on us, and I can wait for you to get there."

"No." She pulled her gaze from his and moved away, before grabbing a long T-shirt from the top of her luggage. "No. I won't."

This was too much. Maybe he didn't want to experience the heartache after all. He was so sure… The hurt started in his chest and spread through his body.

"We don't need to," she said, before he could find a response.

His thoughts slid like socks on linoleum, unable to find purchase. "What?"

"I'm moving back here."

Agony flipped to hope and lifted his heart. "What?" He still couldn't manage anything more intelligent.

"I haven't told anyone yet. I decided last night. This is home, and Atlanta isn't. I've fought it for so long, but being back here… I miss it. I miss Liz and getting to know my little sister… And I'd miss you."

That was closer to what he hoped to hear. Fuck. This was a million times better, in a lot of ways. "Move in with me," he said. It was impulsive, like so much of his time with her, but it felt right.

"Ian…" She still didn't look at him. "What if it doesn't work out? You're putting a lot of everything into this."

"I'm not worried. If it falls apart, it'll be a hell of a ride. But it won't. We'll be amazing together. I love you, and you love me." He wasn't sure about that last bit, but he had a pretty good feeling it was true.

"You're that certain?" Something was off about her voice.

He climbed from the bed. "Yes." He knelt in front of her and realized she wore a giant grin

She met his gaze. "You're an arrogant ass. You know that, don't you?"

Relief filled him. "I've heard it before."

"You're right, though. I do love you. I hate the idea of not knowing when or if I'll see you again. And I can't give you up."

Hearing her say the words buoyed him in a way he didn't think possible. He felt so light he might float away. "Is that a *yes*, to the moving in?"

"And a tentative *yes* to the merger. And a God-damn-fucking-straight I want to see you tonight."

He knotted his fingers in her hair, rose to eye level, and crushed his mouth to hers until she was the only thing in the world. When they broke apart, it was with a gasp.

She laid soft kisses along his mouth. "You really should get to work." Her tone was light and playful.

"I am. Have your lawyer call mine?"

"You say the sexiest things. And okay."

This was insane. All of it impulsive and unplanned and completely open to go wrong. Ian wasn't worried. As he studied Mercy—her bright gaze, her flushed and swollen lips—he'd never been more certain he was doing the right thing.

* * * *

One month later

Mercy resisted the urge to adjust her stockings. Again. The pencil skirt felt too tight, the matching jacket too restrictive in the shoulders, and the silk shirt underneath was suffocating.

Liz said she needed to look nice, though. As much as Mercy put on a bold face and insisted over and over she had this covered—she could do professional—she was still terrified. Last time this much anxiousness filled her, eighteen-year-old her

215

was hopping on a plane to South America and leaving her past behind.

She licked her lips, but it didn't help bring the moisture back into her mouth. It wasn't as though she thought this was a bad idea. The opposite. She struggled to believe it had gone so well up to this point. The contracts were in place, the details ironed out, and her attorney assured her she didn't surrender any autonomy in this deal.

One of the paralegals led Mercy and her lawyer into a conference room, and Mercy's pulse hammered in her ears. Ian already sat at the table, next to his own representative. Seeing him helped relieve some of the tension, especially with the smile he flashed her as everyone shook hands.

A notary and witnesses were there. It was Mercy's understanding that this type of paperwork was usually signed with the interested parties in separate rooms, at different times, and everything was assembled afterward. She wanted Ian with her, though. His presence was comforting, despite the stuffy professional atmosphere sucking the life from the air.

For the next hour and a half, people pointed at signature lines, skipped over so much of the relevant information in their contracts, and asked them both to pen things. She knew what was in the documents; she'd scoured them for weeks.

When it was all done, her wrist ached, and the adrenaline coursing through her had dulled to a raw gnawing in her gut.

People shook hands again, congratulations were passed around, and Ian's lawyer told him he could have the room if he needed to finish anything up.

The moment the door closed after the last person, leaving Ian and Mercy alone, she slumped into her chair in relief. Checks needed to clear escrow—she was assured it was only a formality—and other behind-the-scenes stuff would still happen, but as far as she knew, it was as good as done. Which also meant Ian's people could deal with this professional, legal, stressful bullshit in the future. Not that she thought the transition would be easy—integrating staff, figuring out logistics—but she looked forward to the challenge.

Ian crossed the room, rolled her chair back a few inches, and rested against the edge of the table, facing her. His smile grew. "So, Ms. Rowe, welcome to Thompson Advertising."

"*Rowe* and Thompson Advertising." She couldn't even pretend to be irritated.

He grasped her fingers and pulled her to her feet and into him. "Of course. How could I forget?"

"With the number of times we went back and forth over naming?" She knew he hadn't even started to. She draped her arms around his neck and slid between his legs. Pressing her body to his was one of her favorite pastimes. She didn't see it ever getting old. The heat, the familiar smell of aftershave and *him*—she didn't know how else to describe it—was all just *right*. "Well, I'm broke until the checks clear. Where are you taking me for lunch?"

He glided his hands down her back and over her ass. When he reached the hem of her skirt, he inched it up, until he brushed her thighs with his fingers. "I thought I'd eat here." He slid higher, to the edge of her panties.

"In the lawyer's office." She sucked in a sharp breath at the teasing contact, and it took all her restraint not to shift her weight enough to grind against his hand.

"No?"

"We should at least make it to the car."

He kissed her hard, holding her close enough his erection dug into her stomach. When he broke away, he didn't let go. "You're going to have to walk in front of me. I can't hide this."

"Whose fault is that?"

"Yours." He shifted his hands to her hips and pushed her back. "But I'll compromise. I'll try and keep my hands to myself, *mostly*, until we're out of the office, *if* I get to cop a feel in the elevator."

"I suppose." She laced her fingers with his and tugged him toward the door. "But only because I would've let you do that anyway."

With his warm palm settled against her skin, and the energy flowing between them—hell, with everything—Mercy's heart felt safe for the first time in her life. It was a better sensation than she ever imagined.

THE END

About the Author

USA Today Bestselling Author Allyson Lindt is a full-time geek and a fuller-time author. She likes her stories with sweet geekiness and heavy spice, and loves a sexy happily-ever-after. Because cubicle dwellers need love too. Learn more about Allyson's books, including signing up for her newsletter, by visiting http://www.allysonlindt.com.